Tanner
The Carmichaels
Leigh Fenty

Chapter One

"Im old enough."

T anner was leading Peso around the training pen in front of an enthralled audience. Five of his nieces and nephews were on the small bleachers, built for them to observe whatever was going on in the pen. They loved watching Tanner. And they were all convinced he could talk to the horses, and the horses talked back to him.

Riley, at fourteen, was the oldest of the group, followed by Thea, who was seven. The rest of them were six, five, and four. The four toddlers were in the house with Ruthie and the full-time, live-in nanny Deacon had hired after his second daughter Emery was born. There were currently nine Carmichael children spread between three sets of parents, with one on the way. The nanny had her hands full when they were all at the house.

Riley called out. "Is he ready to be ridden?"

Tanner stopped Peso and ran a hand down his side. "Well, let's find out." The horse had yet to be saddle broke, but Tanner had gotten him to take a bit last week. Tanner gathered the reins before jumping up and putting his weight on the horse, balancing on his chest on Peso's back. The horse took a few steps, then stopped and glanced back at Tanner, as if it were an everyday occurrence.

Tanner slid down and smiled. "Yeah. There you go. Aren't you the calm one?" He looked at the kids. "Okay. Here goes."

He shortened the reins even more, grasped a handful of Peso's long black mane, and jumped as he threw a leg over the horse's back. Tanner settled onto Peso's bare back, then leaned forward and whispered in his ear. "Good boy." He sat up, and gave the horse a little squeeze. Peso took a small jump, then started walking, and Tanner led him around the pen. After a full circle, he urged him into a trot. The horse continued to act like this wasn't the first time he had a rider on his back. "Good job, Peso."

The children knew not to cheer around a green horse. So they all clapped silently as their uncle circled the pen. He tipped his hat at them and went around again, this time at a lope. Peso was a smooth ride and Tanner loved the feeling of a strong powerful animal under him without a saddle in between him and the horse. He felt it was the best way to communicate and let the horse learn exactly what was expected of him.

At the sudden sound of a horn honking, Peso startled and the smooth ride was over. He forgot about the man on his back and reared up at the obtrusive noise. Before he had a chance to react, Tanner found himself on the ground. He hit hard, landing on his back, and it momentarily knocked the wind out of him. He laid still for a moment, and tried to catch his breath. Riley jumped off the bleachers and headed for the gate, but Tanner held out a hand as he sucked in some air.

"Stay there. I'm okay." He took another moment, then got up slowly to make sure he wasn't hurt, and dusted himself off. He picked up his hat before approaching Peso, who was still nervous and shied away from him at first. "Hey boy. You're okay." He glanced in the direction of the sound. "It's just a very rude visitor in a pickup truck." Peso let him approach, and Tanner rubbed his back and side. After a few moments, he calmed down and nuzzled Tanner's palm.

Tanner left Peso in the pen and headed for the barn and the strange truck parked in front of it. The kids all climbed down from the bleachers and followed him. As he approached the truck, a woman stepped out. She had a mess of short, wavy blonde hair that seemed to do whatever it pleased, and a pair of light purple glasses perched on her nose. They were the same color as the few random streaks of purple in the woman's hair. She definitely seemed out of place on a ranch in norther Texas.

Tanner scowled at her. "You can't be honking your horn around the horses." He slapped at the dust on his jeans. "You made my horse dump me in the dirt."

"Oh, I'm sorry. I didn't realize. I was just trying to get someone's attention."

"Well, you got it."

She pushed away a lock of hair that had fallen across her glasses. It was a strand with purple in it and it blended into her glasses.

Tanner tried to lose the scowl. "No harm done, I guess. It's not the first time I've hit the dirt."

"Are you Tobias Carmichael?"

The kids all giggled, and Tanner and the woman both glanced at them standing in a bunch a few feet behind him. "No. I'm Tanner. Tobias is my brother. Why are you looking for him?"

"He called me about his horse."

"And who are you?"

"Dr. Harper Waverly." She stuck out her hand.

Tanner hesitated before giving her a brief shake. "You're the new vet?" She didn't look like a vet. She seemed too young and a little frazzled. And somehow too pretty, but he wasn't sure why that would exclude her from being a vet.

"Yes." She glanced at the kids again, who were unabashedly staring at her. The three boys and two girls were all wearing boots and cowboy hats. The youngest girl was also wearing a princess dress, and had a tiara perched on the crown of her pink hat.

Tanner turned to them. "That's it for the day, guys. Head on back to the house." He watched them until they got to the porch, then he looked at the doctor again.

She smiled at him. "That's quite a fan club you have."

"My nieces and nephews."

"Big family."

"There are four more girls who aren't old enough to be out at the pen."

"Wow. Prolific family." Tanner glanced at her and she backtracked. "It's great. Really. I didn't mean anything."

"I suppose the sheer number of them can be a shock. But they are spread between three sets of parents."

"And you don't have any of your own?"

"No. Not married. And no plans to do so." He couldn't help but notice her eyes were a deep brown, almost black. He nodded toward the barn. "Tobias should be inside with Chance."

Tanner headed for the barn while Harper got a leather bag out of the truck. When he went in, he met Tobias on his way out.

"Have you seen the damn vet? She was supposed to be here an hour ago."

Harper stepped up beside Tanner. "Damn vet, at your service." She held out her hand to Tobias. "Dr. Harper Waverly." Seeing her standing next to his six-foot-three brother, Tanner realized just how short Harper was. She couldn't be more than five-five or five-six.

"Right. Sorry." He shook her hand. "Tobias Carmichael."

She looked at Chance, who was tied outside of a stall. "Is this the patient?"

Tobias walked over to him. "Yeah. This is Chance. Dr. Benton told me a couple of years ago he was getting some arthritis in his front legs. But it seems to have gotten worse, and he's not eating very well."

Harper pushed her bag into Tanner's available arms, earning another scowl, then knelt and felt Chance's front legs. "They're pretty hot." She stood. "Can you walk him around for me?"

Tobias led Chance around in a circle. Then stopped and patted his neck. "Good boy."

Harper went to Chance again. "He's definitely favoring them. Especially the left." She glanced at Tanner, and took the bag from him. "You need to ice his legs. Thirty minutes on and an hour off. Do it tonight and see how he's moving in the morning." She dug in her bag and pulled out a small bottle with a dry powder in it. She handed it to Tobias. "This is Mountain Arnica. Make a paste and rub it into the joints tonight after his last ice bath."

"You're prescribing herbal medicine?"

"Yes. I firmly believe in a holistic approach whenever possible."

Tobias looked at her. "Really?"

"Yes." She took something else from her bag. "And this is frankincense and glucosamine. Give it to him orally twice a day."

"You can't be serious."

She gave him a small smile. "Will you try it? If he doesn't improve, I can always give you pharmaceuticals."

Tobias frowned at the two containers. "Fine. When will I see some improvement?"

"He should start eating better by tomorrow afternoon. If he's not. Call me."

Tobias glanced at Tanner, who raised an eyebrow, then shrugged and nodded. "Okay. We'll give it a shot."

"Thank you."

Tobias looked at her for a moment. "I'm sorry if this is a rude question, but how long have you been a vet?"

"Two years."

"You don't look that old."

"I'm old enough."

He nodded. "Right. I suppose you are."

"One more thing. Can you lift his hoof for me? Let me look at his shoes."

Tobias lifted Chances right front hoof and Harper checked out his shoe. "A corrective shoe might help."

"Corrective shoe?"

"A bar shoe. Do you have a farrier?"

"Yes. One of our men does all the shoeing."

"If you like, I could work with him and we can see if we can make this guy more comfortable by spreading out his weight a little."

"Okay. I'll let him know." Tobias offered his hand, and Harper shook it. "Thanks."

"You're welcome. Thank you for being open to trying something non-traditional."

"Well, as someone who has spent a fair amount of time in pain, I'm all for ulterior methods to pharmaceuticals."

"I'll check in with you tomorrow, then."

"You have a good night, Dr. Waverly."

"Please. Call me Harper."

"I'll talk to you tomorrow, Harper."

She and Tanner left the barn, and he walked her to her truck.

"How long have you been in town? Last I heard, Dr. Benton was having trouble finding a replacement."

"I got here last week. He's been taking me around and introducing me to the various ranchers, but we haven't made it out to you yet."

"Well, welcome to Connelly."

"Thank you."

"This is the Starlight Ranch. You'll be spending a fair amount of time out here."

"Do you have a lot of sick animals?"

"No. Mostly routine stuff. Shots and such."

"Right. Of course." She got into the truck. "I'll be seeing you then, I guess."

Tanner tipped his hat. "Yes you will."

She turned the key in the ignition and nothing happened. She tried again, then looked at Tanner.

Tanner moved to her window. "Is there a problem?"

She gave him a small smile. "It won't turn over. Are you a mechanic, by any chance?"

"No. I can change a tire and put gas in the tank. But that's about it. I'd much rather work with horses."

She picked up her phone. "I'll have to call someone." She glanced at him. "Is there a mechanic in town?" She frowned at her phone, then got out and held it up in the air.

"If you don't have the local cell service, you won't have much luck making a call. Especially out here."

"You're kidding." She walked away from the barn as she kept an eye on her phone, apparently not trusting the word of the man who'd lived there his entire life.

"Nope."

She sighed and dropped her phone to her side. "So I can't even call a taxi or an Uber?"

"Um...Uber?"

"Never mind. I forgot I was in the middle of nowhere."

"Yeah. We don't have taxis either."

"How do you get somewhere if you break down or just don't want to drive?"

"Everyone knows everyone. You wait long enough on the side of the road and someone is bound to come by and give you a lift."

"Two problems with that. I'm not on the side of the road. And I don't know anyone."

"Wrong. You know me." Tanner took out his phone and called one of the hands. He smiled at Harper when she reacted to his phone working just fine.

"Mr. Carmichael?"

"Hi, Hank. Do you have a minute to look at a truck? The new vet's here to check on Chance and her truck won't start."

"Sure. I'll be right there."

Tanner stashed his phone. "One of my men will come take a look at it. He keeps everything with an engine running around here."

"Thank you. You've been very helpful. I appreciate it."

"No problem. We're a friendly lot around here."

Tobias came out of the barn and walked over to them. "Still here?"

Tanner spoke up. "Her truck won't start."

"Did you call Hank?"

"He's on his way."

"Okay, if you've got this handled, I'll go track down my wife and the boys." He tipped his hat at Harper. "Thanks again."

"Of course."

She looked at Tanner. "You two don't look that much alike."

"I'm the odd man out. I take after our mother's side of the family. Blond, blue eyes." He decided to leave out several inches shorter than his brothers. He figured she probably noticed that.

"I see."

"The good-looking side of the family."

She nodded and looked as though she didn't get his joke, then said, "Oh, right."

"So, yeah. Hank should be here any minute now."

Chapter Two

"You've heard of the Hatfields and the McCoys?"

Hank finally showed up after an awkward fifteen minutes. When he opened the hood and started poking around, Harper looked at Tanner.

"I'm sure you have things to do. You don't have to wait around."

"Oh. Yeah. I guess I should put Peso away." He glanced toward the training pen, then back at Harper. "Just keep your hand off the horn until I get him in the barn."

She held up her hands. "I won't get near it."

Harper watched him as he went to the training pen and approached the horse. The horse seemed reluctant to come to him at first, but finally walked toward Tanner. The man seemed to have a way with horses. And he wasn't too bad on the eyes, for a cowboy. She wasn't particularly fond of cowboys. But here she was living in cowboy country, tending to their horses. It's not the life she'd planned for herself. But it was the life she currently had. She would embrace it as best she could.

When Hank cleared his throat, she stopped watching Tanner and turned toward the man who hopefully would get her truck going.

"Battery's dead miss. And I expect it's shot."

"So I need a new one?"

"Yes. Stan at the hardware store can fix you right up on Tuesday."

"Tuesday? That's four days from now."

"Yes, miss. Everyone is closed this weekend for the holiday."

"Holiday?"

"The Fourth of July, miss."

"Oh, right. But that's on Monday."

"We like to take full advantage of the holidays around here. The fourth being on Monday is a good excuse for a three-day weekend."

"I see. Thank you for your diagnosis."

"My pleasure, miss."

He walked away as Tanner approached, leading the horse. He stopped in front of the truck.

"Bad news?"

"Bad battery."

"Oh, damn. Stan will fix you up on Tuesday."

"Right. So I heard. And what am I supposed to do until then?"

"I can give you a lift back to town as soon as I put Peso away."

"Can I leave it here overnight until I can find someone to tow it out of here tomorrow?"

"Of course. Leave it here until Tuesday. No need to haul it into town. We'll just push it out of the way."

"Well, I suppose I don't have much choice."

"Do you need anything out of there?"

She went to the truck and took out another bag and her purse. "I guess this is it. Are you sure you don't mind?"

"Positive. I have to head home, anyway. Towns not too far past my house. I'll be right out."

He headed to the barn and Harper found herself watching him again. She shook her head. *Geez, stop.*

Tanner came out a few minutes later and headed for his truck. She followed him and got in as he started the engine. "Well, at least mine started."

She looked around the surprisingly clean truck, considering it was owned by a dusty cowboy with mud on his boots. "Yours is slightly newer than mine."

He drove down the tree-lined drive, then turned onto the small two-lane highway that would take them to the town of Connelly.

She glanced at him. "So, you don't live at the ranch?"

"No. Well, yes. I live on the ranch, just not there at the main house. About seven years ago, we took over the O'Hare ranch. Two years ago, after Winston passed, I moved his house. My sister and her husband and I train horses there."

"I see. And where do they live?"

"They have property not connected to the Starlight. He's a Fremont. And well, when you've been around a while, you'll hear all about the Fremonts. He's the prodigal son, so to speak."

"Hmm. Small town drama?"

"You've heard of the Hatfields and the McCoys?"

"Yes."

"Well, the Carmichaels and the Fremonts are kind of like them. Without the guns."

"Wow. Okay."

"Just to be clear, though, this feud is only in Leo Fremont's head. None of us know what it is he has against us. But it's been that way for as long as any of us can remember."

"Maybe because his son is married to your sister."

"No. It was going on long before that." He slowed down when he saw a deer on the side of the road. "So, where'd you come from?"

"Austin."

He laughed. "Both my sisters-in-law are from Austin."

"I'll have to meet them."

Another deer jumped from the trees and ran out in front of them. Tanner slammed on the brakes, but still bumped the deer with his left front bumper. The deer was knocked to the ground, but got up and scampered off.

"Damn deer."

"Pull over. We need to see if she's okay."

"Seriously?"

She scowled at him. "Yes. Seriously."

Tanner pulled to the side of the road and parked. As Harper got out of the truck, he took a flashlight from the glove box. The sun was going down, and it'd be dark soon. He left the truck and followed her.

"Hold on. Don't go traipsing through the woods after an injured animal."

"She's not going to hurt me."

"Just let me go first."

She studied him for a moment. "Fine."

He went in front of her and they continued into the brush. "We're never going to find her. She must not be hurt bad if she took off like that."

Harper put a hand on his back. "Shhh." He stopped and looked at her and she asked, "Do you hear that?"

"I don't hear anything."

"Over there." She stepped in front of him and followed the sound Tanner still couldn't hear. They found the injured deer lying under a tree. It tried to get up as they got close, and Harper stopped walking.

Tanner held up his hand. "Let me."

"Let you what?"

"Just...stay put." He looked at the frightened deer. She had a cut on her leg, but it didn't seem life-threatening. He took a step toward her. "Hey there. We're not going to hurt you. We're here to help you." The deer looked at him and seemed to calm down. "There you go. Can I come sit by you while Harper looks at your leg?"

He glanced back at Harper, who was staring at him in disbelief. He shrugged. "I have this thing with animals."

"I see that."

He took a couple more steps toward the deer. "Good girl." He moved in close and knelt next to her. "That's a girl." He reached for her and stroked her side. He talked to Harper without losing eye contact with the deer. "You can come over now."

"Are you sure?"

"Yep. She and I are in tune."

Harper moved toward the deer and knelt next to Tanner. "This is pretty unbelievable. You know that, right?"

"I've never tried it on a deer. But it seems to work."

Harper took some things out of her bag and dressed the deer's wound while Tanner continued talking to it. When she was finished, she glanced at him.

"What now?"

"Get up slowly and walk away." She did, and Tanner got to his feet. "We're going to leave you alone now. You should be fine."

He backed up to Harper and after a few moments, the deer got to her feet and ran off.

Harper took his arm. "How'd you do that?"

"I've always had a way with animals. Mostly horses, but I guess it extends to all God's creatures. Though I don't know that I'd want to try it on a bear or a cougar."

"Well. I'm amazed. That was a beautiful thing to watch. You should've become a vet."

"I actually thought about it when I was younger. But too much school. I didn't want to leave the ranch." He started walking. "We should get back. It's almost dark."

Harper followed him. "Thank you for helping me fix her up. She might've been fine. But she also might've gotten an infection. She'll be fine now, though."

When they got into the truck, Tanner looked at Harper. "When I acted like I didn't want to go after her, it wasn't because I didn't want to help her. I just figured we'd never find her."

She smiled. "It's obvious you like animals. I didn't think badly of you."

"Okay. Good." He started the truck and pulled back onto the road. "Keep an eye out. If we have to save anymore deer, we'll never make it to town."

When they got to town, Harper directed Tanner to the house she was renting. He pulled into the drive and looked at the house.

"The old Sutter place."

"Excuse me?'

"Old man Sutter lived here for about forty years. We were always afraid of him when we were kids. He was our token creepy guy."

"I see. And what happened to Mr. Sutter."

"Um...you don't want to know."

"Oh no. I do." She turned in her seat. "Tell me."

"He died."

She looked at the house. "In there?"

Tanner nodded. "I'm sure they bought a new bed."

She closed her eyes. "Oh my God, so gross. I'm sleeping on the couch tonight."

He laughed. "Really, they had to have gotten new furniture. He was... Well, you'd know if it was left from him."

She put her hands to her ears. "Stop talking, please." She opened the door and got out, then leaned in and said, "Thank you for the ride."

"No problem. Um... If you need a vehicle to use over the weekend. We can loan you one. We've always got a spare or two lying around."

"That's really nice. But I couldn't."

"What else are you going to do? Most of your patients can't be brought into the office. Although there probably won't be too much going on this weekend."

"So it sounds like you celebrate big here."

"Yeah. Any excuse to take a few days off."

"What's going on this weekend, then?"

"The farmers' market and craft fair is tomorrow. Sunday is the rodeo and chili cookoff. On Monday morning, the parade. Then the town dance with fireworks at ten or so."

"Sounds...interesting."

"It is. You should check it out. Get to know the folks of Connelly. They'll all be your customers sooner or later."

"I'll think about it. And I'll call you tomorrow and let you know if I need to borrow a truck."

"Okay. Have a good night, Harper."

"Like that's going to happen now."

She watched Tanner drive away, then went inside her house. She had to sign a year's lease to get it, which was fine. She figured she'd be here at least that long. She needed to build up some experience and hopefully start persuading people to at least try her holistic approach. The big veterinarian practices in Austin didn't take too kindly to her way of doing things. That and the fact she was only twenty-four seemed to be a big turnoff for established clinics. Here, she was her own boss. She had no one to answer to except her patients and their owners. Dr. Benton had told her it might be a hard sell around here. But she was confident she could win them over. She'd just convinced the Carmichael family to give her herbs a try. That had to be a big win.

She sat on the couch and her cat Shadow jumped up and laid next to her. She petted his gray fur. "You'd think people would be impressed by the fact I finished vet school at twenty-two."

Shadow began purring. "I know. You appreciate me."

She looked around the furnished living room. "Please be new furniture."

Chapter Three

"I'm not dead, yet."

W hen Tanner got home, he noticed Skyler's truck parked by the barn, and he went to see why he was still there.

Skyler was standing by the foaling stall watching their mare, Lucy, who was due to deliver anytime. Tanner came up beside him.

"How's she doing?"

"I'm a little worried about her. I thought she would've delivered by now. Or at least started to labor."

Tanner entered the stall and patted Lucy's neck, then ran a hand down her side and felt her belly. He looked at Skyler. "She's not in labor yet."

"Did we do the math wrong?"

"No. It's not a precise number. She'll deliver when she's ready. She's not stressed. She's perfectly calm and wondering why she's in this nice big stall."

"I guess."

Tanner left the stall and patted Skyler's back. "Go home to Abby and the girls. I'll keep an eye on Lucy."

"Are you sure?"

"Yes." He grinned at Skyler. "I swear you're more nervous about Lucy's impending delivery than you were when Abby had the twins."

"Don't tell her that. It's just that this is the big one. We've invested a lot of money in this already and the damn foal isn't even here yet."

"Thunder and Lucy are going to produce a perfect baby. All the money we put into this union will be worth it."

"Our first Andalusian."

"It's going to be fine. I'll stay here tonight and keep an eye on her."

"Will you call me if she goes into labor?"

"Yes. And if she doesn't, then you can sleep in the barn tomorrow night."

"Deal."

Tanner walked Skyler to his truck. "Go get some sleep. It's bound to be a long weekend."

Skyler got into his truck, and with a wave, headed down the driveway. Tanner returned to the barn and went to Lucy's stall.

"I'm going to go get something to eat. I'll be back. You chill in your fancy stall."

Lucy nodded her head and stomped the ground with her foot. She was a beautiful horse, and they'd paid a small fortune for her and their stud. If all went well, they'd join the elite few who bred and sold Andalusians in the U.S.

He went to the house and into the kitchen. Ruthie kept him pretty well supplied in meals to warm up, and he rarely had to cook anything from scratch. He took a container of chili out of the refrigerator and put it in a pot on the stove. It was from a large batch she'd make for the chili cook-off on Sunday. There was a cook-off three times a year, and Ruthie won the most votes every time. She, hands down, made the best chili in northern Texas.

While he waited for it to heat, he gathered a pillow and some blankets to take to the barn. He had a cot there he'd used many times. He was used to spending the night in the barn if one of the animals needed someone to watch over them. He didn't mind. He found it quite peaceful, once the horses all settled down and the only sound was their rhythmic breathing.

His dog Rider scratched at the kitchen door, and Tanner let him in.

"Hey, buddy. I bet you're hungry."

Rider was a lab mix. The mix being a mystery. They'd only had a few dogs when he was growing up. Deacon figured he had enough to worry about without adding a dog or two to the mix. Tanner understood that. But as soon as he moved into Winston's house, he got himself a puppy. Living here, just the two of them, they'd developed a deep bond, and Tanner welcomed the company. Without Rider, his first few months alone in the big house would've been very lonely.

Tanner put some food in Rider's bowl, then brought the pan to the table, along with a spoon. He didn't like to do dishes, so he avoided using them whenever possible. When he was the only one eating, there was no reason not to eat right out of the pot.

He threw some grated cheese on top and some diced onions, then sat down to his dinner. Rider finished his food and came to lie under Tanner's chair. He was the cleanup crew, in case something hit the floor.

After he finished, Tanner ran some water in the pot and set it in the sink. He gathered his bedding, and he and Rider went out to the barn. He found Lucy calmly eating some hay. Tanner doubted she was going to foal tonight. But he'd stay with her to make sure she was alright. He made up his cot, then picked up the old guitar he also kept in the barn. He wasn't a good player, by any means, but he played well enough to keep the horses entertained. When the weather was unsettled and the horses were nervous, he'd come play for them. If it was really bad, he'd sing. But his singing was worse than his guitar playing. Deacon was the only one in the family with a good voice. And he only sang in the shower.

Tanner started playing, but stopped halfway through the song when Rider came to attention to something behind him. He turned to see Deacon coming into the barn. Rider ran to him and got a pet.

"Serenading the horses again, I see."

"I thought maybe I could lull Lucy into going into labor."

"Let me know if it works. I'll have you play next time Cassidy gets pregnant."

"Seriously? Four isn't enough?"

Deacon laughed. "My wife loves kids. What can I say?"

"Maybe you'll have a boy next time."

"At this point, I don't know if I'd want one. Besides, I watch my sweet girls next to Tobias' wild and crazy boys, and I'm fine being a girl dad."

"I'm not sure if sweet describes Emery. I love her, but she's a bit stubborn. And she holds her own with her cousins."

"That's for sure. She can't quite decide if she wants to be a cowgirl or a princess."

"No law saying she has to make a choice."

"True enough. But since she's thick as thieves with Grady and Jordan, and pretty fond of her Uncle Tanner, she just might grow up to be a bronc rider. Of course, I'd prefer she became a championship jumper like her other two uncles." He went to Lucy's stall, and she came over and nuzzled his hand. "She sure is a beautiful horse."

"Skyler's scared to death something's going to happen and he'll disappoint you since he talked you into the Andalusian breed."

"It didn't take much to convince me. We're going to do really well with them. Who wouldn't want to own a horse like this?"

"I've been working with Thunder. Trying to make him a little more manageable."

Deacon turned to him. "Be careful. If he just does his job, that's good enough for me."

"I know. But it'd be nice to be able to handle him. His original owners never did a thing with him but let him breed. That's all he knows."

Deacon laughed. "Lucky horse."

Tanner shook his head. "Wow. That's something I'd expect Tobias to say, not you."

"I'm not dead, yet." He patted Rider's head. "So, you going to be alright here tonight?"

"Yep. Me and my trusty dog."

"And a barn full of horses."

Tanner gave him a smile. "Thanks for checking in."

"I know it's been two years now, but I still miss you, kid."

He shook his head. "You see me every day."

"Yeah. But that's not the same as having you sleeping down the hall."

"I had to leave the nest at some point."

Deacon nodded. "I never did."

"No. But it's your nest now. And you've been filling it up with little Carmichaels."

"That I have. Speaking of which. I need to get back. It's story time."

Tanner frowned at him. "I don't believe you ever read me a bedtime story."

Deacon thought about it for a moment. "That's because Abby insisted on doing it. She read to you every night until you were ten. You about broke her heart when you told her you were too old for stories on your tenth birthday."

"I remember that. I don't remember her being broken-hearted though. Seems to me she said something to the effect of, 'It's about time you stopped being a baby.'" He looked at Deacon. "Oh shit. I broke her heart."

"She got over it."

"I'm going to have to apologize to her."

"Don't bother. You've more than made up for it over the years."

"Hmm. Maybe."

Deacon headed for the door. "I'll see you tomorrow. Call me if anything happens tonight. I'd like to see this beauty being born."

"I will."

Deacon left, and Tanner picked up the guitar again. "Okay, Lucy, any requests?"

*****

Tanner slept fairly well, considering he spent the night on a cot in the barn. When someone giggled near him, he opened his eyes to see one of the twins' face a few inches from his.

"Geez." He tried to focus. "Gillian?"

Abby came up behind her and picked her up. " This is Gianna. Sorry, Tanner. She got away from me."

Skyler stepped up, holding Gillian.

Tanner yawned and then frowned. "I don't know how you guys tell them apart." He sat up. "Why are you all here?"

Skyler set Gillian down. "We came to stay with Lucy. You have to be at the street fair, right?"

"Oh sh..." He glanced at the girls. "I forgot. What time is it?"

Abby smiled. "You need to be there in thirty minutes."

Tanner stood and stretched. "Just enough time to change and make a cup of coffee."

Abby took his arm. "You change. I'll make you some coffee and warm a muffin or something."

Tanner looked at her. "You're going to warm me up a muffin?"

"I'm not totally useless in the kitchen." She pointed at Skyler. "Do you have something to say about that?"

"No, ma'am. I've got the girls. Go ahead."

As Abby and Tanner headed for the house, he glanced at her. "Seriously. How do you tell them apart?"

"It's the eyes."

"Really?"

"No. I'm their mother. Of course I can tell them apart. They're totally different."

"No, Abby, they're not. And I remember when they were babies, you painted their toe nails different colors, so you didn't get them mixed up."

"True. But now they have personalities and very subtle differences."

"Okay. Whatever."

"The Wexler sisters. You could tell them apart."

"Well, sure. They were totally different. They wore their hair different and wore completely different clothing."

"One of these days, you'll see the difference. Deacon and Tobias can tell them apart."

"Yeah. I don't buy that. I think they just keep getting lucky with guessing."

They reached the kitchen door and went inside.

"You go change. I'll make coffee. Do you have any pastries from Ruthie?"

"Yeah. In the fridge."

He headed for his bedroom and got changed. He considered shaving, then just combed his hair and put on his favorite hat. He could smell coffee as he approached the kitchen.

"You do know how to make coffee."

She went to the microwave and pulled out a muffin on a plate. "I also know how to use the microwave."

Tanner took the muffin from the plate. "Do you know how to wash a plate?"

She set it in the sink. "It'll be waiting here for you when you get home."

He picked up the travel mug she'd filled with coffee. "You guys help yourself to whatever."

"Thanks, we always do."

"I know."

"Have fun selling hotdogs. Just remember, it's for the kids."

"Right. That's the only reason I'm going."

Chapter Four

"Do you have a problem with hotdogs?"

As Tanner got to the park and was walking to the booth, he got a text message.

"*Hey. I can't make it. Got a sick kid. Hope you can handle it yourself.*"

"Dammit." He tucked his phone in his pocket.

When he got to the booth, Melissa was there setting it up. They'd gone to school together and were still friends.

"Hey, Tanner."

"Morning. Are you here to help?"

"No. I'm just helping with the setup. I need to be at the beer garden when it opens at noon."

Tanner frowned. "That's in an hour."

"Sorry. Brett's coming right?"

"No. He texted me. Says his kid is sick."

"Oh, no. I hope it's nothing serious." She smiled at him. "You can handle it." She was trying to hang the banner the Junior Rodeo Logo on it.

He stepped up to help her. "Probably. It's just a lot easier with two people."

"It's only four hours." She looked around the booth. "I think it's all set up. You just need to get the dogs going."

"You sure you can't stay for the first hour?"

"It's not even going to get busy until noon. Besides, I told Teddy I'd help him set up the bar."

"Fine. Thanks for setting me up, at least."

She smiled at him. "You're welcome. Come have a beer when you're done here."

"Yeah. Maybe."

He watched her walk away. She'd been pretty obvious about the fact she'd like to get to know him better. But he wasn't interested. Her brother Teddy worked for Leo Fremont and, for some reason, thought the guy was great. He'd picked up Leo's animosity toward the Carmichaels and made it quite clear he didn't like Tanner and his family. Dating Melissa would be asking for trouble.

He filled the hotdog roller with hotdogs, then set out the mustard, catsup, and chopped onions at the end of the table. He put the change he'd gotten at the bank yesterday in the cash box and looked around the booth. It seemed he was ready.

Unfortunately, Melissa had been wrong about it not getting busy until noon. By eleven-thirty, there was a line of about ten people. Everyone was patient, but Tanner was barely keeping up with it.

When he noticed a familiar face standing to the side of the line, he smiled. "Dr. Waverly."

"Good morning." She nodded toward the line. "Looks like you could use some help."

"My booth buddy didn't show up." He smiled at the man waiting to order. "Four dogs, Ben?"

"Yes, please, Tanner. And a dog with no bun for Charlie here."

Tanner looked over the table at Charlie the Dachshund. "Hey Charlie. How are you today?"

Charlie wagged his tail as Tanner went to prepare the hotdogs. When he brought them back, along with four sodas and four bags of chips, Harper was petting Charlie.

When she stood, Tanner looked at her. "Do you have to be somewhere?"

"No. Are you trying to get rid of me?"

"No. I don't suppose you'd like to help me out? At least until this line goes down a little. You kind of owe me for the ride and all. Not to mention causing Peso to dump me in the dirt."

"Wow. I'll help. But you only get to use that once."

"I'd really appreciate it." He took the next order and while he was putting the dogs in the buns, Harper came into the booth.

"Just until the line goes down."

"Thank you." He delivered the hotdogs, then turned to her. "Not much to it. Five dollars for a hotdog, a bag of chips, and a soda. If they just want the hotdog, two bucks."

"Easy enough."

"And as you take dogs off the roller, replace them. That way, we won't run out."

"Got it."

"Thank you for helping."

"You told me to come hang out and meet people. I guess this is as good of a way as any."

Harper jumped right in and was doing great until a family with four kids came up and the father order dogs for all of them.

She cocked her head. "Are you sure there isn't something healthier for the kids to eat?"

Tanner smiled at the father. "Coming right up, Tom." He took Harper's arm and led her to the hotdog roller. "We're here to sell hotdogs, not judge the people who buy them."

"Sorry, you're right."

"Do you have a problem with hotdogs?"

"Other than the fact they're highly processed meat loaded with chemicals and some many other unhealthy things, no."

Tanner stared at her. "Don't hold back. Tell me what you really think about them." He fixed five hotdogs and brought them to Tom. "Sorry about the doc, here. She seems to have a hotdog prejudice."

Tom laughed. "Why is she working the booth, then?"

"Just helping me out."

When the line cleared out for a few moments, Harper looked at Tanner. "Doesn't the Carmichael family have enough money? Why are you hocking hotdogs?"

"This isn't a family booth. It's the Junior Rodeo booth. The money goes toward scholarships and after-school programs. It gives the kids something to do besides get into mischief after school and on the weekends."

"Were you in the Junior Rodeo?"

He adjusted his hat. "Yes. And high school rodeo."

"And adult man rodeo?"

"Yes, that too. I ride broncs on occasion."

She looked surprised. "Really. You seem too smart for that."

"Do you have a problem with rodeo, too?"

"I think it's kind of mean to the animals."

"You feel sorry for the wild horse trying like hell to toss the cowboy onto his ass in the dirt? More like onto his head. Or the bull who wants to kill the guy on his back."

"If I was a bull, and some cowboy wanted to ride me, I'd be mad, too."

Tanner laughed. "Okay. Wow. How'd you end up here?"

"I was offered the job."

"Hmm." It seemed Dr. Hart was anxious to find a replacement.

"What's that supposed to mean?"

"I think you're in the wrong town, Doc. Maybe the wrong state."

"Well, you're stuck with me for a while."

When Tanner saw Deacon, Cassidy and the kids come up to the booth, he left Harper and went to them.

Deacon was carrying Luna, and he smiled. "How's it going?"

"It's been busy until the last few minutes."

Deacon nodded toward Harper, who'd come up to them. "Are you going to introduce us to your helper here?"

Tanner glanced at her. "She's the new vet, Harper Waverly. Harper, this is my brother Deacon, his wife Cassidy and their kids, Thea, Emery, Kinsley, and baby Luna."

Harper shook with Deacon and Cassidy. "Nice to meet you." Emery was once more wearing a dress with her cowboy boots and tiara decorated cowboy hat and Harper smiled at her. "I love your outfit."

Emery giggled. "Thank you."

Tanner spoke up. "Harper's from Austin."

Deacon raised an eyebrow. "Really. Seems to be a pattern."

Harper smiled. "How so?"

He glanced at Cassidy. "Oh, Cassidy and our sister-in-law are both from Austin."

"Tanner did mention that."

Tanner looked at her, then back at Deacon. "She stepped in to help me because Brett bailed on me."

"I see." Tanner was pretty sure Deacon didn't see.

"So, hotdogs?"

Cassidy shook her head. "No. I think we'll get something a little healthier."

Harper cocked her head at Tanner.

Deacon took out his wallet. "But we'll add to the pot." He handed Tanner thirty dollars. "How's Lucy doing?"

"Skyler and Abby are with her. When I left, she still hadn't gone into labor."

Deacon switched Luna to his other hip. "She'll deliver when she's ready."

"I know. I'm just getting anxious." Luna held her arms out to Tanner and he took her from Deacon.

"Maybe you should have sung to her a little longer last night."

Tanner smiled. "Yeah. That's probably it." He kissed Luna on the cheek, then handed her back to Deacon. They left and Tanner looked at Harper, who was smiling at him. "You sing to the horses?"

"Only when they're restless or about to deliver."

"You have a horse in foal?"

"Yes. A very expensive horse. We're all a little anxious for her to get on with it."

Harper leaned on the table. "What kind of horse is she?"

"An Andalusian. We got a mare and a stud last year. This will be our first foal."

She straightened back up. "I love those horses. I've never been near one, though."

"Well, you're welcome to come take a look anytime you want. She's a beauty."

"Can I come watch her deliver?"

He wanted to say no, but she seemed so excited at the prospect. "If she ever does, sure. It couldn't hurt to have a vet on standby."

She took his arm for a moment, then let go. "Thank you."

"I'll be going back home at two when I get out of here. You can come with me, if you want."

"I'd love to."

"Okay, then."

They served a few customers, then had another lull. Tanner fixed himself a hotdog and Harper scowled at him.

He walked over to the condiments. "What?"

"Do you know what's in those things?"

He squirted mustard on his hotdog then sprinkle chopped onions onto it. "No. And I don't want to know. I like hotdogs and I'm not going to let you ruin it for me."

"Okay. Suit yourself."

"I will. Thank you." He took an oversized bite and chewed it with exaggeration. "Mmm." He talked with his mouth still full. "So good."

She turned away from him. "You're really gross and immature."

She served a few customers while he finished his hotdog. When he opened a can of soda, he held it up to her. "I suppose you have a problem with this, too."

"Only the fact it has ten teaspoons of sugar plus caffeine."

"You have something against caffeine, too?"

"Yes."

He took a drink of the soda. "So no coffee?"

"Of course not."

"Wow. Are you a vegetarian?"

"I'm vegan, actually."

He kind of knew what that meant. "So…"

"I eat no products from something with a face."

"You really are in the wrong state. You realize you've moved to the middle of cattle country, right? The land of big steaks, ribs, hamburgers."

"I realize."

He set his can down and folded his arms across his chest. "What do you eat?"

"Fruits, vegetables, nuts, beans. I do just fine."

"Hmm. When's the last time you had meat?"

"Never. My parents are vegan."

He dropped his hands to his side. "Wow. So how do you know you don't like it if you've never tried it?"

She shook her head. "It's not a matter of taste. It's a lifestyle choice. I choose to be healthy. And I choose not to kill animals to feed myself."

A customer came to the booth and Tanner went to take their order. Dr. Waverly was going to have a hard time assimilating into the town of Connelly.

They got another rush and were busy for the next thirty minutes. When it slowed down again, Tanner gave Harper a smile.

"If you want to go walk around a bit. I think I can handle the last hour?"

"Are you trying to get rid of me?"

"No. I'm just—"

"I'm kidding. I'm hungry, but I'm sure there's nothing here for me to eat."

"There's a booth selling corn on the cob somewhere. And those fries that are like one whole potato."

She raised an eyebrow.

"Oh right. Fries are bad." It sounded really good to him, though. "Why don't you go get yourself some corn and bring me back some fries?" When she looked at him, he added, "Please. And I'll buy."

He took a ten out of his wallet and held it out to her. "What do you say? You eat corn right. Or is the fact they call it an ear of corn a problem?"

She snatched the bill from him. "I eat corn."

"The booth should be the next row over."

"I'll find it."

Tanner watched her weave her way through the crowd. She wasn't like anyone he'd ever met. Which was interesting, but a little too scary. She and he had nothing in common.

Chapter Five

"So many Carmichaels."

Harper returned fifteen minutes later with fries for Tanner and two corns on the cob for herself. She handed him the fries.

"Here is you heart attack waiting to happen."

"I'm twenty-six. I think I'm good for a while." He ate a few fries, then licked his fingers.

She shook her head. "At the very least, you should weigh a lot more than you do if you eat like this all the time."

He picked up a napkin and wiped his mouth. "I work hard. And I don't eat like this all the time. It's the Fourth of July."

"It's the second of July, but whatever. Are you saying you cook healthy meals for yourself?"

"No." He ate another fry. "The family cook makes healthy meals for me. Of course, they include meat, so you may not consider them healthy."

"You have a cook?"

"Not me personally. She's been with the family since before Deacon was born."

Harper set her paper plate down and picked up a piece of corn. "Hmm."

"What's that supposed to mean?"

"Nothing." She leaned on the table and started in on her corn.

He watched her for a moment. "I'm not going to apologize for having money. Our family has worked hard to get where we are. No one handed it to us."

She shrugged. "That's not what I meant. Just as someone who never had any money, it must be nice, that's all."

"You had enough money to go to vet school. That can't be cheap."

"Scholarships." She took another bite.

"Really?"

"Yes. Full ride. All eight years. Only it didn't take me eight years."

He pointed at her. "I knew you weren't as old as you should be two years out of school. How old are you?"

She looked at him for a moment before answering him. "Twenty-four."

"Seriously?"

"Why? Do you think I look older than that?"

"No. You look twenty-four." He cocked his head. "Are you like super smart?"

She sighed and took another bite of corn. "Yes."

"How smart?"

"Do you want my IQ?"

"No. How long did it take you to get your degree?"

"I graduated from high school at sixteen. Finished vet school at twenty-two."

"Wow. Impressive. Here I thought I was smart by having my AA when I graduated high school."

"That's not bad. Did you go to college?"

"Nope. I was set to go to Yale. Both Deacon and Tobias went there. But Deacon finally realized I had no interest in going and I was more valuable here working with the horses."

"Your brothers went to Yale?"

"Yeah."

"What about your sister?"

"She went to Southwestern for a year and a half. Then our mother died, and she came home and told Deacon she wasn't going back."

She studied him for a moment. "Why does Deacon get to make all the decisions for you and your family?"

"He's been running things since our father died eighteen years ago."

"Okay. He couldn't have been very old at that point."

"Twenty-three. Can I eat my fries now before they get cold? Or would you like me to go back a few generations on the Carmichael family tree."

"You can eat."

He ate some more fries, but was interrupted by a customer. Harper held up a hand. "I'll get it. Keep eating your fries." He watched her as she took the order for four hotdogs, then another order for two. She was only supposed to stay until the line was under control. Here it was three and a half hours later and she was still there.

When the next shift showed up to relieve Tanner, he looked at Harper. "So, you still want to come see Lucy?"

"Yes. Please."

They walked through the crowd, heading to the parking lot. But before they got there, Tanner stopped at a booth selling oatmeal cookies. He stopped and bought two of them.

Harper shook her head. "You're still hungry?"

"They're not for me. They're for my nieces."

"Don't you have a bunch of them?"

"Yes. But only two will be at the house when we get there."

They arrived at the truck, and Tanner opened the truck door for Harper.

She smiled at him. "You're pretty polite."

"I was just raised right."

"I guess you were. Can we stop by my house on the way through town? I'd like to have my bag with me."

"Sure. I guess it couldn't hurt to be prepared."

They stopped at Harper's house, and Tanner waited in the truck for her. She came out ten minutes later with her medical bag and a jacket.

Tanner nodded toward her jacket. "It's ninety degrees out."

"I know. But tonight it'll be seventy-five. I like to be prepared."

"Right. Are you planning on staying the night in my barn?"

"If Lucy doesn't deliver today. Maybe I can hear you serenade the horses."

"Yeah. That's not going to happen."

They drove through town, then another five miles to the horse ranch and Tanner's house. He parked in front of the house and they walked to the barn. Harper looked around.

"Wow. Very impressive. Is that an indoor arena?"

"Yeah. We train jumpers and a little dressage."

"So, you jump?"

"Me? Not so much. But Skyler and Abby are pretty good. Skyler was a champion rider a few years ago. And Tobias almost went to the Olympics."

"Almost?"

"He got hurt right before the trials. He was pretty messed up for a while."

"It seems you have a very talented family, Tanner."

They reached the barn and went inside to find Skyler sitting on the cot. He looked up and gave them a smile as he stood.

Harper smiled at him. "I'm Harper Waverly. The new vet."

"Oh right. Tobias was telling me about you." He shook her hand. "Skyler Fremont."

"The prodigal son."

"Excuse me?"

"Sorry. Tanner's words, not mine. I didn't mean anything." She went to Lucy's stall. "She's beautiful." She glanced at Tanner. "Can I go in?"

"Sure. Give her a professional assessment."

Harper opened the stall and went inside. She approached Lucy, then rubbed her nose before moving down her neck and side. Finally, she felt Lucy's stomach.

Skyler glanced at Tanner and raised his eyebrows.

Tanner scowled and shook his head.

Harper looked at them. "Can you hand me my stethoscope?"

Tanner opened her bag and took out the stethoscope, and brought it to her. She took it from him and listened to Lucy's belly for several minutes from various spots. She finally stood and smiled at the men.

"She looks good. The foal's heartbeat is nice and strong."

Skyler leaned on the gate. "Is she in labor yet?"

"I'd say she's in pre-labor. She's a little restless. Has she been eating?"

"Not in the last hour or so."

"I think she's getting ready. It shouldn't be too much longer now."

Tanner sighed. "Finally."

Abby came into the barn holding a baby monitor. "The girls are asleep." She noticed Harper when she came out of the stall. "Oh, hi."

Harper smiled at her. "Hi. You must be the sister."

"Yes. I'm Abby."

"Harper Waverly."

They exchanged a handshake. "The vet?"

"Yes."

"Very nice to meet you. I love your hair."

Harper ran a hand through her hair. "Thank you."

Tanner and Skyler exchanged a look.

Abby went to the stall. "How's she looking?"

Skyler stepped up next to her. "Doc says she's getting close."

"Oh yay. Should we call Deacon and Tobias? I think they want to be here for the delivery."

Skyler looked at Harper. "Do you have a time frame?"

"A few hours yet, if she keeps progressing."

Tanner took out his phone. "I need to go to the house for a minute. I'll call them."

Abby turned to him. "Don't wake up the girls."

"I won't. I've been an uncle for a while now. I know not to wake up a sleeping child."

———— ❧ ————

Tanner left, and Harper smiled at Abby. "So three brothers, huh? That must've been fun growing up."

"Fun? Actually, I couldn't ask for better brothers. They're the best. Have you met them all?"

"Yes. And Cassidy, is it?"

"Yes. Deacon's wife."

"I guess the only one I haven't met is Tobias's wife."

"Gemma's great. You'll meet her soon enough. She's been a little under the weather."

"Nothing serious I hope."

Abby smiled. "Morning sickness. She's had three kids. No morning sickness. This one she's been sick since before she even knew she was pregnant."

"Goodness. I hope she gets over it soon."

"She thought, and I think, kind of hoped it was because it was a girl. But they had an ultrasound. It's another boy. Number four."

Harper shook her head. "So many Carmichaels."

"I know. It's kind of crazy. I think Deacon and Tobias are trying to outdo each other."

Tanner came back in the barn with a sixpack of beer and a sandwich.

Harper scowled at him. "You're eating again?"

Tanner ignored her and offered a beer to Skyler, then looked at her. "Beer?"

She shook her head. "No thanks."

"You don't drink beer, either? I assure you no animals were harmed during the brewing of this beer."

"I only drink wine and only very occasionally."

Tanner shook his head. "Man, you don't have any fun at all."

Abby nudged him. "Hey, leave her alone."

"She doesn't eat meat or drink coffee. Now no alcohol?"

Abby looked at Harper. "Ignore him."

"I've been trying to all day."

Tanner raised his hands. "Whoa. I've been a lot nicer to you than you've been to me today."

Lucy whinnied and stomped her foot, and Abby went to the gate. "You two, hush. You're upsetting Lucy."

Harper stepped up next to Abby. "She's getting restless."

"It's okay girl. I know it feels like your insides are being turned inside out, but trust me when I say this, you will get through it."

Skyler came and kissed Abby on the temple. "You would know."

Tanner sighed and sat on the cot to finish his sandwich. He opened a beer and took a sip. Harper glanced at him, then turned back to the horse. She had to admit he was pretty cute. He was also pretty annoying.

Skyler turned to Tanner as he took a sip of his beer. "Did you get the guys?"

"Yeah. They'll be over in an hour or so."

Abby laughed. "It's going to be a party."

Chapter Six

"Oh, boy. Here we go."

When Deacon and Tobias arrived, Lucy's labor had progressed. She was lying in the hay, and Abby and Harper were in the stall with her. Tanner was giving Skyler a guitar lesson to pass the time.

Deacon walked up to the stall. "How's she doing?"

Harper was sitting next to Lucy, and she looked up at him. "Won't be long, now."

Tobias came up next to Deacon. "She seems to be pretty calm."

Abby stroked Lucy's side. "Just like she knew what she was doing."

Harper nodded. "Well, they generally do. She just probably wondering why we're all here bothering her."

Deacon put a hand on Tobias' shoulder. "Let's give her some privacy." They joined Tanner and Skyler by the cot.

Tobias watched them for a moment. "You know, you might have better luck learning from someone who actually knows how to play the guitar."

Tanner scowled at him. "I've been playing awhile, brother. And you don't play at all, so..."

"I could if I wanted to. I just prefer the piano. And I'm a damn good piano player."

"Yeah. Only because Deacon hogtied you to the piano bench three afternoons a week."

"How would you know? You were in preschool at the time."

Deacon looked around the barn. "About nine years ago, I spent the night here with Cassidy waiting for Precious to be born. We had our first kiss that night."

Tobias turned to him. "I thought your first kiss was at the school."

"No. Right here in the barn."

Tobias folded his arms across his chest. "Cassidy didn't break up with me until after Precious was born."

Deacon pointed at him. "Right. About that."

"So you kissed her when she was still technically going out with me?"

Tanner started laughing. "Oh, boy. Here we go."

Deacon raised his hands. "No. It wasn't like that. It was a spontaneous thing. And she broke up with you as soon as it happened."

Tobias raised an eyebrow. "I ought to kick your ass for lying to me for the last nine years."

Abby called from the stall. "Guys. Behave. Nobody is kicking anybody's ass over something that happened a decade ago. Tobias, you ended up with who you were supposed to end up with, right?"

"Yeah. Of course." He grinned. "I'm just messing with him. Cassidy told Gemma years ago. And she told me."

Deacon shook his head. "Bastard."

Harper stood. "Can everybody calm the hell down? This foal is about to make an appearance."

The four men went to the gate and watched as Lucy delivered the foal. Once she got to the final stages, it went fast. She delivered a colt who was the same color as the stud—chocolate brown with a cream mane and tail. The colt laid in the hay to get its strength back, and a few minutes later, Lucy got to her feet and went to nuzzle him.

Deacon smiled. "It's always beautiful, no matter how many times you see it."

Tanner noticed Harper wipe away a tear. "You okay there, Doc?"

She glanced at him. "Yes. This is actually the first birth I witnessed this close."

Tobias laughed. "Well, if you stay around, it certainly won't be your last."

Harper and Abby left the stall to give Lucy and her colt some bonding time alone. And they all backed up a little from the stall.

Abby hugged Skyler. "Our first baby Andalusian."

He kissed her, then shook hands with Tanner, Deacon, and Tobias. "Thank God it all went well."

When the colt got to his feet, they all watched him wobble for a moment until he got his balance. Then he walked slowly to his mother and started nursing.

Deacon smiled. "Okay, Harper. You get to name him."

"Me? It's not my horse."

"No. But it's your first up-close and personal birth. And the first person to see the foal gets to name him."

"But we all saw him at the same time."

Tanner went to her and nudged her. "Just give the damn baby a name."

She went to the gate and watched the colt for a few minutes. When Tanner came up next to her, she glanced at him. "It's really hard. I want it to be perfect. Is he going to be a stud?"

"Probably not."

"How about El Primero?"

"The first?"

"Yes. Is that okay?"

"It's great." He looked at the others. "Good, right?"

They all nodded in agreement.

Harper turned to them. "If it's stupid, you can tell me."

Tobias laughed. "It's not stupid. He's the first Andalusian born on the ranch. It's very fitting."

She smiled. "Good. Thank you for letting me name him."

Tobias patted Deacon on the back. "We should get back."

Deacon took his phone out to take some pictures of the colt. "Everyone is going to want to see pictures." He took several before stashing his phone. "Okay. Congratulations, you guys. Skyler, you did good."

"I've been sweating this for the last year."

Tobias and Deacon left, then Skyler and Abby prepared to leave.

Tanner grinned. "Don't forget your children."

Abby hugged Tanner. "Don't worry. We won't. I can't believe they slept this long."

Skyler sighed. "Now they'll be up all night."

Abby stepped back from Tanner. "Will you keep an eye on Lucy and El Primero tonight?"

"Of course."

Tanner shook with Skyler, then they left after thanking Harper for being there. Tanner and Harper went to the gate and watched the horses.

She turned to Tanner. "Thank you for letting me experience this."

"Of course. I can take you home whenever you're ready."

"Would it be okay if I stayed a while longer? Just to make sure they both keep eating."

"Sure. Are you hungry?"

"Yes. All I've had to eat since breakfast was those two ears of corn."

"And let me guess. For breakfast, you had tree bark and grass."

"How'd you guess?"

"Come on. Let's go see if I have any food without a face on it in the refrigerator."

They left the barn. "The food doesn't have a face. The animal it comes from does."

"Whatever. You know what I meant."

They went in the kitchen door and Harper looked around. "This is nice."

"Did you think it wouldn't be?"

"Well, seeing as you're a bachelor and all." Rider came running in from the living room, and she knelt to pet him. "Aren't you a handsome boy?"

Tanner watched her. She was obviously a dog person. She rubbed his ears and gave him kisses, then looked up at Tanner.

"Sorry. I really love dogs."

"I can see that."

She stood and Tanner went to the refrigerator. "I think there might be a spinach salad in here."

Harper came up behind him and peered over his shoulder. "That's a lot of food. All prepare and ready to eat? Your cook really does take care of you."

He glanced back. She was standing really close to him. But he didn't mind. "Ruthie loves me."

She took a couple of steps back. "How sweet."

He took out a bowl with spinach salad in it and handed it to her. "Spinach, almonds, strawberries."

"Perfect. Thank you."

He took out a bowl of beef stew for himself. "Potatoes, carrots, onions...Oh, and fresh Carmichael beef."

He put the bowl in the microwave to heat while Harper sat at the table with the salad. He got her a fork, then took the stew out and brought it to the table. He set it down, then got a loaf of Ruthie's bread and set it in the middle of the table with some butter. He sat down and buttered a slice of bread and held it out to her.

She shook her head and took a plain piece.

Tanner nodded. "Right. Butter. Comes from cows. You know it doesn't hurt the cows to milk them. In fact, they're pretty miserable if they don't get milked."

"But you're still exploiting them."

"Exploiting them?" He took a bite of stew. "You've been brainwashed, lady."

"Brainwashed? By Whom?"

"By your parents. By your...people."

"My people? Just because it's different from the way you were raised, it doesn't mean it's wrong."

"Not eating a good steak or some perfectly cooked bacon is wrong. Living on greens and nuts is wrong. I don't care what you believe or what you say. You'll never convince me..." He held up a piece of beef. "...that this is bad for you." He put it in his mouth. "Mmm."

She took a bite of spinach. "Mmm."

"People have been raising animals to feed themselves for...a really long time."

"That doesn't make it right."

"Yeah, well. It doesn't make it wrong, either."

"Great argument."

Tanner dug into his stew. There was no getting through to her.

They got through dinner without any further discussions about Harper's lifestyle choices. And when they were finished, they returned to the barn. El Primero was nursing again, which was a really good sign.

Harper went to the gate. "Are you staying out here tonight? Or are you just going to check on them periodically?"

He glanced at the cot. "I'm going to sleep out here."

"Play some guitar?"

"Maybe."

"Do you want some company?"

He looked at her for a moment. "Um...sure. You want to stay?"

"If you don't mind."

"I don't mind." He honestly didn't. Which surprised him.

"Okay. Then let's hear some guitar music."

"No."

"Come on. Don't be shy."

"I'm not shy. I'm just not going to play in front of you."

"I heard you playing with Skyler. You're not bad. One song. I promise I won't make fun of you if that's what you think I'm going to do." She picked up the guitar and handed it to him.

He sighed. "Fine. You're going to bug the hell out of me until I do."

He sat on the cot and started playing an old country song. When he got to the first chorus, Harper started singing. Tanner was surprised she knew the song. And amazed at how good her voice was. She stood at the gate and sang to the horses with her back to him. When he got to the end of the song, she turned to him.

He set the guitar down. "You sing."

"Why is that so surprising?"

"It's not, I guess. More unexpected. How do you know that song? I didn't think anyone knew it except Deacon and my dad."

"My grandfather used to sing it to me."

"Huh. What do you know?"

Harper smiled. "You're not bad, yourself. Do you only play for the horses?"

"Who else would I play for?"

She shrugged. "I imagine the country ladies around here would swoon at the sight of a cowboy playing his guitar."

"Not a whole lot of swooning going on in Connelly. Guitar playing cowboys are a dime a dozen."

"I suppose they are." She walked over to him. "So, what are we going to do until bedtime?"

"Why do we have to do something?"

"We can't just sit here for the next three or four hours."

Tanner thought for a moment. "We could play cards or something."

"Do you have a chess board?"

"I'm not playing chess with you."

"Why not?"

"Because you're obviously a super brain."

"That doesn't mean I'm good at chess. And it sounds like you're plenty smart, too. If you'd gone to college, I don't think it would've taken you four years to get your degree."

"Probably two."

"So. Do you have a chess board?"

"I'll go get it."

Chapter Seven

"It looks like we're having a sleepover."

An hour into the game, neither of them had an advantage. They were evenly matched, and it didn't seem the game was going to end anytime soon. Tanner made a move, then got to his feet to check on the horses. Both of them were sleeping peacefully. Harper came up beside him and rested her arms on top of the gate.

"If you want to go sleep in your bed, I'll gladly stay here with them."

He scowled at her. "I'm not letting you sleep out here by yourself. I can still take you home."

"I don't want to go home. And I don't need you to protect me in this perfectly safe barn."

"That's not what I meant."

She put her hands on her hips. "What did you mean?"

He took a few steps back away from her. "I meant that if anyone should sleep out here, it should be me. It's my barn, after all. I have no doubt that if anyone tried to come in here and mess with you, they'd very quickly regret it."

"I'm not sure if that's a compliment or an insult."

"Take it however you want." He returned to the chessboard, which they'd set up on a barrel with a wooden stool on either side. "Can we save this game for another time? I'm having trouble concentrating. And I don't want you winning because I was too tired to think."

"Sure, whatever makes you feel better about yourself."

"Wow." The woman was impossible.

She smiled as she left the stall and walked toward him. "I'm kidding. There's only one person who's ever beat me at chess. So, I'm actually impressed."

"So, you *were* trying to hustle me."

"Not hustle. It's not like we put money on the game." She grinned. "Although it's not too late to make a little wager."

Tanner shook his head. "I'm not betting with you on who will win."

"Okay. Whatever. We'll pick this up next time I'm here."

He perched on the stool. He should insist she go home. Why was he letting her stay? She was annoying and if she stayed, he'd have to give her the cot and he'd be sleeping on the floor. He'd get no sleep, and then he'd have to deal with her in the morning when he was sleep deprived.

He figured he might as well give it another try. "Are you sure you don't want me to take you home?"

"Are you trying to get rid of me?"

"Kind of, yeah."

She moved to the cot and sat down. "If you want me to leave, just tell me."

He pointed at her. "That would be rude."

Harper laughed. "You're way too polite, Tanner. You're the sweet baby brother, aren't you?"

"Actually, yes. And I'm fine with that. We all have our role to play." He went into the small office in the barn, which was used more for storage than doing any paperwork. But it had a refrigerator that always had beer in it. He took one, then returned to his stool. "I think I'm going to need one of these to get through the night."

"If you really want me to go home, I will. But take me now before you drink that beer."

Tanner looked at the bottle, then opened it and took a drink.

Harper nodded. "Okay. It looks like we're having a sleepover."

Thirty minutes later, Tanner was trying to get comfortable on the floor of the barn. He'd brought some more blankets from the house and a two-inch foam pad, but it didn't do much to protect him from the hard wooden floor. And even though he swept the floor before he laid his padding down, the hay was still hanging in the air around him and making his nose itch.

He rolled onto his back. "I should've had another beer."

"I don't know why you won't just go into the house and sleep in your bed."

He was quiet for a moment as he listened to the sounds of the horses around him. "Who is the one person who can beat you at chest? Or I should say one other person. Because I will beat you."

"My brother."

"Is he smart, too?" Tanner heard her move on the cot.

"He makes me look like the village idiot. He graduated from MIT when he was nineteen."

"Wow."

"Yeah."

"What's he doing now?"

"He's in medical research, genetics. Crazy advanced stuff that I don't understand."

"Huh."

Tanner rolled onto his side and put a hand on Rider, who was lying next to him. The dog sighed in utter contentment. *At least one of us is comfortable, buddy.*

Harper woke up when she heard Tanner talking quietly to Lucy. He'd set a flashlight on its end. It dimly lit the ceiling above him and made just enough light to see by. Harper could make out his shoulders and head. He was stroking Lucy's nose and talking to her.

"There you go. It's okay. Your baby's just hungry. You need to relax and let him eat."

Lucy fussed for a moment, then seemed to give into Tanner's soothing voice. Harper couldn't see the colt, but by the expression on Tanner's face, she could tell Lucy was allowing him to eat.

"That's a good girl." He continued to stroke Lucy's nose until the colt finished nursing. "Okay. Time to rest. I really need to get some sleep." He kissed Lucy's nose, before leaving the stall. He retrieved the flashlight, and as he went to his bed, he noticed Harper up on one elbow.

"Sorry. Didn't mean to wake you."

"You kissed her."

"So?" He knelt next to his bed, then laid down. "I like horses."

"Is she okay?"

"Primo's nursing was freaking her out a little. The guy's an aggressive eater."

"Did he get his fill?"

"Yeah. They should sleep for a while now."

She laid back down and he turned off the flashlight. "It'll be light in a couple of hours. Best get some more sleep."

She heard him rustle around for a few minutes, trying to get comfortable. Stubborn man. She felt a little guilty taking his cot. She kind of forced herself on him. He had this covered, and he didn't need her sticking around. She knew she annoyed the crap out of him and it was fun. But she'd go home in the morning and leave the poor man alone.

Harper woke up to Tanner swearing, and when she opened her eyes, he was standing over his bed and taking his shirt off. He dropped it on the floor and scratched his back.

He was quite buff in a working cowboy sort of way, and she was distracted for a moment. When she cleared her head, she asked, "What's wrong?"

"Damn hay."

She smiled, and he glared at her. "I need to go shower. Can you make sure Lucy and Primo are okay?"

"Yes. Go shower."

He picked up his shirt and headed for the door. She watched him go. "Wow. Not bad, for a sweet baby brother."

She checked on the horses, then shook out Tanner's blankets before folding them up and stacking them on the cot. When she heard a vehicle pull up outside the barn, she went to see who it was. She expected to find a Carmichael, but it was an older man in a very fancy truck with a matching horse trailer.

He got out and gave her a smile. "Good morning. Who might you be?"

"I'm Harper Waverly. The new vet in town."

He shook hands with her. "Hope you're not here on business."

"Not officially. I came to watch their mare deliver last night."

He took a few steps back and rested a hand on the hood of the truck. "Oh. Okay. I was looking for Tanner, actually. Is he around?"

"He's in the house. I'll go get him."

"Thanks. I'm a couple of hours early."

"I'll send him out."

Tanner let the water hit his neck and run down his back. He was tired from two nights of sleeping in the barn. But he had a full day. Which would start in a couple of hours. He had time to eat a decent breakfast and finally take Harper home. It was long overdue. He'd been with her for almost twenty-four hours. Twenty-four really long hours.

When the bathroom door opened, he said, "What the hell?"

"Sorry. I called through it, but you didn't answer."

"Close the damn door."

Harper closed it, leaving just an inch open. "There's someone here to see you. He looks important. A client maybe."

"What's he driving?"

"Big black truck with an even bigger black horse trailer."

Tanner sighed. "With a silver horse logo on the side?"

"Yes. Do you know him?"

Tanner turned off the water. "Max Porter. He's two hours early."

"He said as much. What do you want me to tell him?"

"Nothing. I'll be out in a minute. Please close the door."

"Right."

Harper closed the door, but Tanner waited a minute before getting out of the shower, half expecting her to open it up again. The woman needed to go home.

He dried off and got dressed, then combed his hair and looked in the mirror. "Good enough."

On his way through the house he found Harper in the kitchen. "I know you don't drink coffee, but do you know how to make it?"

"Yes."

"Would you please make me a cup and bring it to me?"

He expected resistance, but she gave him a smile and said, "Of course."

"And help yourself to whatever. There's some fruit in the fridge."

"Thank you."

He headed for the door, but stopped before going out and turned back to her. "I'll get Max's horse situated, then I'll run you home."

"Okay."

She was being awfully cooperative. "What's up with you?"

"Nothing. Go see your guy. I'll make your coffee."

He wasn't convinced. But he nodded, then left through the kitchen door.

Max Porter had a troublesome horse, which he hoped Tanner would be able to help him with. The two men shook hands.

"Sorry I'm so early. I got him loaded up faster than I thought. He usually gives me hell as soon as he sees the trailer. Once we got him in, I didn't want to dawdle. I didn't even want to stop to eat breakfast."

"It's fine. Let's get him out of there."

Max opened the rear of the horse trailer and the big chestnut gelding looked back at Tanner with a mixture of fear and distrust. When Tanner stepped into the trailer, the horse got restless and started shuffling his feet and bobbing his head.

Tanner approached him from an angle. He didn't need to be kicked by a crazy horse this morning. When he got close, he put a hand on the gelding's hindquarters. The horse jumped at his touch, and Tanner looked at Max.

"He's on edge. Is he always this skittish?"

"He was always a little high-strung. But it's much worse now. I can barely get near him."

Open both doors, then back the hell up. I'll bring him out.

Tanner went into the stall next to the horse. "What's his name?"

"Chester."

Tanner put a hand on Chester's back and slowly moved it toward his neck.

"Hey there, Chester. What's got you so hot and bothered? I'm not going to hurt you. And I hope to hell you don't hurt me. That'd ruin my day." He leaned in and whispered to the horse. "I just spent twenty-four hours with Harper. So give me a break."

The horse looked at him and stood relatively still while Tanner release his lead line. He clicked his tongue. "Okay. Back it up." He put a little pressure on the rope and the horse took a couple of steps back. "There you go. A few more steps, then you can turn around and we'll walk right out of here."

Chester backed out of the stall and Tanner turned him to face the back of the trailer. "There's your exit. Nice and slow now." The horse was still nervous, but he seemed to know freedom lay on the other side of the doors. He let Tanner lead him out. But once he cleared the trailer, he tried to rear up.

Tanner held firm on the lead line and Chester looked at him. Tanner smiled. "I'm not putting up with your shit, Chester." Tanner led him to the small training pen and took him inside. Max came up behind him and closed the gate.

"Well done, young man."

Tanner looked at him. "Why don't you go get yourself some breakfast in town? Give me some time to get to know Chester."

"Okay. I'll be back in an hour."

Tanner looked at him. "Make it two."

Chapter Eight

"I'm usually a little more tactful."

Tanner let the horse off the lead, then left the pen. He leaned on the fence and watched him, and the horse stared at him from the far side.

Harper came up beside him. "I see why they call you the horse whisperer." She handed him a travel coffee mug.

He took a sip. "I think it's going to take more than whispering to get this guy in shape."

"What's wrong with him?"

"The question is what happened to him? Max says this is new behavior. Horses don't become ornery for no reason."

"Do you think he was mistreated somehow?"

"I don't know. It may not have been intentional. I'm not accusing anybody at this point." He watched the horse for a moment. "Will you walk around the pen toward him? Nice and slow. I want to see what he does. Don't look at him or talk to him."

Harper started walking around the outside of the rail toward Chester. When she got within twenty feet of him, he trotted away.

"Keep going."

Harper continued around the pen, and Chester kept moving to keep the distance between them. When he took his eyes off of Harper for a moment, and noticed he was getting close to Tanner, he left the edge of the pen and went to the center. He stopped there and stared at Tanner.

Harper completed the circle and came back to Tanner. "What did that tell you?"

"That it's not just me he doesn't like." He turned to her. "I know I said I'd take you home, but I wasn't expecting Max so early. You can take one of the trucks, though. I'm sure you're ready to go home."

She nodded. "Yeah." She looked at Chester. "I don't suppose you let me watch you for a little while. I promise I'll be quiet and not annoy you."

Tanner wondered if that was even possible. He sighed. "Fine. But not a word, unless I ask you something."

"I promise."

He nodded toward the stands. "Go sit."

She held up a finger.

"What?"

"You haven't eaten breakfast."

"The coffee is enough for now."

She nodded, then headed for the small bleachers. Tanner watched her climb to the top and sit down, then returned his attention to the horse. He watched Chester for another ten minutes while he finished his coffee. Then he set his cup on the bottom row of the bleachers and put on his gloves. He took the lead line and lunge whip, then went into the pen.

Chester shied away from him and trotted to the far side of the pen. Tanner went to the middle of the pen and stood still, then started talking to the horse. After a few minutes, he took a step toward him while continuing to talk to him. Chester stayed where he was.

After five minutes, Tanner got close enough to hook the lead line to Chester's halter. He backed up the length of the rope, then snapped the whip behind Chester. The horse took a hop, then started trotting.

Harper was fascinated by Tanner's ability to handle the skittish horse. After thirty minutes of circling the pen, the horse started listening to Tanner's demands to stop and start. An hour later, Tanner was riding the horse bareback around the pen.

But when Max returned and approached the pen, Chester spotted him, stopped short, and reared up. When his front feet landed, he kicked his back feet straight out behind him. Tanner stayed on through the first part, but was thrown off during the rear kick. He hit the dirt and Chester kicked again, barely missing Tanner's head, then ran to the far side of the pen. Max and Harper both went to the gate.

Tanner sat up. "Don't come in. I'm fine." He sat for a moment to get his breath back and let the ringing in his ears subside. The horse's problem was obviously Max. When he went to stand, he felt a sharp pain in his left arm. He got his feet under him and looked at Max.

"I need you to go to your truck until I get the lead off of him. I don't want him to get tangled up in it."

Max nodded and retreated to his truck. Tanner looked at Chester. "What the hell, man? I thought we were friends."

Chester threw his head and stomped his foot. Tanner took a step toward him. His leg hurt too, but it was the type of pain that'd go away soon. The arm was another matter. He continued slowly moving toward Chester, who stayed put. After a few minutes, Tanner reached him and removed the lead. Then he limped toward the gate and Harper opened it.

"Oh my gosh, you're hurt."

"I'm okay." He hung the rope over the railing, then went to the bleachers and sat down with a groan.

"You're not okay. Did you hurt your leg?"

Tanner sighed. "My leg is fine. But I believe my damn arm is broken."

"Well, crap."

Tanner looked at her and smiled. "Yeah. Crap." He looked at Max, who was still hovering by his truck. "I need to go talk to him."

Harper took Tanner's good arm and helped him up. He glanced at her. "Now I'm ready to accuse someone."

When they approached, Max looked properly concerned. "Are you hurt bad, son?"

Tanner walked up to him. "Why is Chester so afraid of you?"

Max took a step back. "I don't know. Like I said, he just started acting crazy a few weeks ago."

"Horses don't start acting crazy for no reason. What happened?"

Max's resolve to insist nothing happen dissolved when Tanner gave no sign of backing down. "You know that big thunderstorm we had a few weeks back?"

"Yeah."

"Well, I'd just brought him back from the farrier and the storm hit. It started pouring, so I made a run for the house and left him in the trailer. I didn't know it was going to thunder and lightning. It was bad, and it lasted a couple of hours. When I finally went out there, he was down in the trailer and scared to death. I barely got him out of there, and he was sure I was there to hurt him. He's been skittish around me ever since."

"He dumped me in the dirt. That's not skittish, that's scared."

"I should've told you the whole story."

"Yeah. You should've. How'd you get him back in the trailer?"

"It took me and my three sons to get him in. We had to blindfold him."

"You never should've put him in a trailer this soon. You might've ruined him forever to load in a trailer."

"Can you help him?"

Tanner looked like he wanted to slap some sense into the guy, but he kept his cool. "You need to leave him here with me. I'll do what I can for him. When he's not so spooked, I'll have you come work with him."

"Thank you. I appreciate that."

"I'm not doing it for you. I'm doing it for Chester. You, I should lock in a horse trailer during the next thunder storm."

Max nodded. "I screwed up, Tanner. I hope you can get him back to his old self."

"I'll do my best." He offered his hand to Max, and they shook, then Max opened the truck door.

"I'll check in with you in a few days."

Tanner nodded, and Max got into his truck and drove away.

Harper looked at Tanner. "You told him what's what."

"I know Max. I'm usually a little more tactful."

"So, let me look at your arm." She took his arm and gently touched it. He winced, and she patted his hand. "Yeah. I think it's broken."

Tanner sighed. "Will you drive me to the clinic?"

"Of course." She looked at the training pen. "What about Chester?"

"He's fine. He's not going anywhere."

They went to Tanner's truck, and he got into the passenger seat. "Dammit. I need to call Skyler. My phone's in the house."

Harper handed him her phone. "Use mine." He cocked his head, and she took it back. "Right. Service."

"I need my wallet. I'll go get it."

"I'll get it. Where's it at?"

"In my room. Will you get it and my phone, please?"

"Yes. Sit tight."

She left him in the truck and went into the house, then took a moment to figure out where his room was. It had to be upstairs. She went up and found his room on the second try. It was surprisingly neat, and she took a moment to look around the minimally furnished room. His bed was made, so props for that. And there were no dirty clothes lying around.

"Okay, Tanner. You're not a slob. That's nice to know." She found his wallet and phone on the small dresser. There was a picture on the dresser of the Carmichael family which included both parents. Tanner looked to be about five or six. It might've been the last family picture taken.

He'd said he took after his mother, and she could see that. His mother was pretty, petite, and blonde. The other three siblings looked like their father. Tall, dark, and very good looking.

It was quite the attractive family. "I see where you guys got it from." She picked up his wallet and phone and went down the stairs.

When she got in behind the wheel, Tanner seemed reluctant to hand her over the keys.

"I'm a good driver, Tanner."

"I'm sure you are. I just don't like anyone driving my truck. I don't even let my brothers drive it."

She held out her hand. "Unless you want to walk to town."

He dropped the keys in her hand. "This is a one-time deal."

"You have to get home."

"I'll be able to drive home once this is set. And after I drop you at your house."

"My house. I almost forgot I had one."

"I haven't."

Harper started the truck without responding and headed down the driveway. Once they hit the road, she glanced at Tanner. "So, how many bones have you broken, bronc rider?"

"Ankle, arm, sprained knee. A couple of concussions. That's about it."

"And you do this...why?"

"For fun."

"Okay. And how many times have you gotten hurt in the training pen?"

"This is the first broken bone. I don't generally fall off in the pen, unless someone honks their horn or a stupid owner gets too close."

She smiled. "Two days. Two falls."

"And what's the common denominator?"

"I didn't cause it today. That was all Max."

He didn't have a response, and he leaned back and closed his eyes for a moment. Harper wanted to keep him distracted. But in a nice way.

"I saw your family picture. How old were you then?"

"Six. That was taken the summer before my dad died."

"That must've been a hard loss."

He glanced at her. "I was seven. I don't really remember him."

"And Deacon raised you?"

"Pretty much, yeah. Ruthie helped."

She smiled. "That's why she loves you so much."

"That and the fact I'm so sweet."

"Well, of course. That goes without saying."

Chapter Nine

"I'm sure you were seventeen once."

T hey made it safely to the clinic and when Harper parked out front, Tanner looked at her.

"Stay here."

"What? No. I'm not staying in the truck."

He could tell there would be no arguing with her. "Fine. Come in. But behave."

"Always."

Tanner raised an eyebrow, then got out of the truck. As they both approached the door, Harper held it open for him. He gave her a slight nod, then went inside. Hallie was behind the reception desk. The boy she'd left Tanner for proved not to be who she thought he was. She broke up with him shortly after moving to Houston, then spent two years going to school, before returning to Connelly. She'd been working at the clinic ever since.

Tanner gave her a small smile. "Hey Hallie."

"Tanner. Are you okay?"

"No. Broke my damn arm."

"Oh no. Go sit, I'll get you signed in. Dr. Hart is with another patient, but he can see you as soon as he's done. Do you want some ice?"

"Um...sure. Thanks." Halley had spent her first two years back trying to get Tanner to go out with her again. But he wasn't interested. She'd broken his heart. He wasn't going to trust her with it again. She was currently dating a local rancher's son. But she didn't seem very invested in the relationship.

Tanner and Harper went to a row of chairs and sat down. A few minutes later, Hallie brought the ice. "Here you go."

"Thanks, Hallie."

She glanced at Harper. "Hi."

Harper smiled. "Hi. I'm Harper. The new vet."

"Oh. Welcome to Connelly." Hallie gave her an insincere smile while she seemed to be trying to determine just what Harper's relationship was with Tanner. When the phone rang, she had to leave.

Harper waited until Hallie was on the phone, then leaned toward Tanner. "So, what's the story between you two?"

Tanner scowled at her. "No story."

"Bull. Come on spill. I'll find out sooner or later, anyway. Small town. Lots of gossip."

He sighed. "We dated in high school."

"Hmm. And you left her for someone else?"

"No. She left me. Moved to Houston."

"Yet, here she is, making eyes at you."

Tanner glanced toward Hallie. "She's not making eyes. And even if she was, I'm not interested. She's damn near engaged. Sort of."

"Sort of engaged, isn't engaged. So, she had her shot at Tanner Carmichael?"

"Something like that."

"I wouldn't think anyone would walk away from a Carmichael. Aren't you a catch, being the last single one?"

"I'm not a catch."

"Okay. Whatever."

"When you're seventeen, you don't think about marrying for money or status. It's all about...never mind."

"No, please. Tell me."

"I'm sure you were seventeen once."

Harper laughed. "Yes, I was. I spent all my time in the library."

"Wow, you must've been a load of laughs."

She scowled at him. "You're kind of mean when you're hurt."

He took a breath. "Sorry. I apologize."

"I've dated. If you're thinking I haven't." She sounded defiant, and he wasn't sure who she was trying to convince.

"I'm sure you have."

Tanner glanced at her and for a second, he almost felt sorry for her. She had spent most of the last eight years in school or trying to prove she was legitimate and worthy of respect from her peers. But she was still stubborn and annoying and it'd take a special kind of man, one with the patience of Job, to take her on.

When the nurse called him back, he was glad for the interruption. "I'm going in by myself."

Harper raised a hand. "I know. I wasn't planning on going with you to hold your hand."

Tanner came out forty-five minutes later with a black cast starting at his elbow and ending at the first row of knuckles on his hand.

Harper got to her feet. "What's the diagnosis?"

"I broke both the radius and whatever the other one is called."

"Ulna."

"Yeah. That."

"I'm sorry. You were pretty stoic for a double fracture."

He glanced toward the door. "Let's get out of here."

They headed for the door, but Hallie came up to them before they could leave.

"Here's your prescription, Tanner."

He took it from her. "Thanks."

She gave him a smile. "Take care."

Harper held the door for Tanner again, then took his arm. "Poor girl."

He held his hand out. "I'll drive."

She stopped and put her hands on her hips. "You have two broken bones."

"It doesn't hurt that much."

She took the prescription out of his hand. "Wow, pretty strong stuff."

"Isn't there some law about you poking your nose into my medical information?"

She handed it back to him. "I'm a doctor."

"You're not my doctor."

"Should we go get that filled?"

"I'll get it filled. You're going home."

"I suppose it's time." She handed him the keys. "You can take me home, then go get that filled. It may not hurt right now, but it will later."

"Gee, thanks for that uplifting news. Aren't you all about natural remedies?"

"Yeah. But sometimes a little pain medication is the only thing that works. Stop being so grumpy. And don't apologize again. Just take me home."

Tanner nodded, then got into the truck. He was quiet while he drove her to the house. When they arrived, she turned to him. "I'm sorry I stuck around so long. It wasn't my intention."

He shrugged. "It's fine."

"Go home and get some rest. Stay out of the pen."

"Yes, ma'am."

She laughed. "Goodbye, Tanner. I'll see you around."

"Bye, Harper."

She went into her house and dropped down onto the couch. She'd been gone for more than twenty-four hours. She thought about Tanner. He obviously thought she was the most annoying person on the planet. But he never insisted she leave. He could've told her to leave several times. He also could've taken her home last night. But he didn't. Why not?

He was cute. There was no denying that. A rich, cute cowboy who loved horses and could communicate with them in a mind-boggling mystical way. And he was cute. Wait, she'd already listed that one. She thought about him without his shirt. Sexy. That's something she could add to the list. Cute, rich, mystical, and sexy. She didn't care about the rich part. He didn't act rich. He acted like a regular cute, sexy cowboy. Oh, and the guitar. He'd said guitar playing cowboys were everywhere in Connelly. But he was the only cowboy she'd heard play guitar. She smiled. "He plays for the horses. How cute is that?"

Tanner decided to get his prescription filled just in case he needed it later. He certainly wouldn't want to drive back into town if he did get to that point. He'd called Skyler and told him what happened, then Skyler must've spread the word, because he'd gotten texts from every one of his siblings and their spouses.

While he waited for the prescription to be filled, he sat in the truck and texted everyone back with the same message. *"I'm fine. Left arm is broken. It won't slow me down too much."*

Almost immediately, the phone started chiming with notifications. He read the messages, but didn't respond. He'd be home soon enough.

When he pulled up to his house, both Skyler and Tobias' trucks were there. He went inside and they were in the living room. He went in and sat on the couch.

Tobias leaned forward in his seat. "What the hell happened?"

"Max's damn horse, Chester, pulled a bronc move on me. I wasn't prepared for it, along with the fact I wasn't using a saddle."

"Well, shit."

"Yeah." He looked at Skyler. "Did you get him into the barn okay?"

"Yes. He was a little skittish, but I coaxed him in with some oats."

"He's going to be a tough one. He spent a few hours in the trailer during a thunderstorm. I may never get through to him."

"Dammit. Max left him in the trailer?"

"Yep. And Chester knows it."

Tobias shook his head. "We should lock Max in a trailer come the next storm."

Tanner laughed. "That's exactly what I told Harper."

Skyler nodded. "Speaking of the doc. Where is she? I half expected her to follow you home."

"Don't even get me started on Dr. Waverly. I finally dropped her at her house. But not until she accompanied me to the clinic."

Tobias grinned. "I think the doctor has a crush."

Tanner shook his head. "No. She just enjoys annoying the crap out of me."

Skyler got to his feet. "Sounds like true love to me." He headed for the door. "Now that I know you're alive and mobile. I need to head home. But I'll check on the horses before I go."

"How's Lucy and Primo?"

"Doing great." With a wave, Skyler left, and Tanner looked at Tobias.

"You don't need to babysit me. I'm fine."

"Nope, I owe you. When I fell off of Esmeralda, you sat with me for hours."

"Totally different. You were messed up." He held up his arm. "This is nothing."

"Still. You must be hungry."

"I am. I haven't eaten yet, today. And I might need to take one of these pain pills, so I should get something in my stomach."

Tobias stood. "I'll go see what's in your fridge."

Tanner had said he didn't need a babysitter, but it was nice to have Tobias there. He was feeling a little bit sorry for himself. His arm was starting to ache now that the adrenaline rush had settled down. He was pretty good with pain. But he didn't like the fact it kept him from doing what he needed to do. What he loved to do. He looked at his cast. It wouldn't slow him down too much, but it'd be a little annoying.

He suddenly wondered what Harper was doing. *Who cares?* He'd be happy if he never saw her again. But of course, that was unrealistic. She was the town vet. He'd run into her sooner or later.

Tobias returned fifteen minutes later with two bowls of stew and some slices of bread. He set a bowl in front of Tanner, then sat in a chair.

"So, tell me all about this annoying lady vet."

Chapter Ten

"I'll just go get that coffee going."

Tobias had stayed for several hours, and after he left, Tanner took a pain pill and fell asleep on the couch. A knock on the door woke him and he sat up and was disoriented for a moment before he realized it was morning. He'd slept all night on the couch. His arm was throbbing, and he had a stiff neck from the angle he'd fallen asleep in. He rubbed the back of his neck.

Rider was lying on the floor in front of the couch. He'd been trained not to bark at someone knocking. But he thumped his tail and let out a little whine.

When the knock came again, Tanner groaned. Anyone he wanted to see wouldn't be knocking. They'd walk right in. He decided to ignore whoever it was and laid back down. But when he heard a familiarly annoying voice say, "Tanner?" he shook his head.

"This can't be happening." He sat and looked toward the door. "Go away, please."

"I'm coming in."

Harper opened the door, and Rider ran to greet her. She petted him enthusiastically and kissed him on the nose before walking to the couch. She took a moment to look at the sorry state he must've been in.

"I've been calling you."

He ran his hand through his hair and sat a little straighter. "I turned my phone off. Why were you calling me?"

"To make sure you were okay." She looked at his rumpled clothes. "Did you sleep on the couch?"

He laid his head against the back of the couch. "How'd you even get here?"

"Your sister gave me a ride."

He lifted his head and looked at her. "Abby brought you here?"

"Yes. I ran into her in town and I told her I'd been trying to get a hold of you, so she brought me out. She's in the barn checking on Lucy and the colt."

"She went straight to the barn? She didn't come see me first?"

Harper cocked her head. "Aww, poor Tanner. She knew I was coming to check on you. She'll be in soon to check on her baby brother."

"Well, now that you know I'm fine, you can leave. Please take one of the trucks. Anyone you want, except mine."

"Abby said you were supposed to compete in the rodeo yesterday."

"Yeah. No big deal. There's always another rodeo."

"I suppose that's true."

She went to a chair and sat down. Apparently, she didn't hear the part about taking a truck and leaving.

She gave him a smile. "So, fireworks tonight?"

"Yes."

"Where does one go to watch the fireworks?"

"To the rodeo grounds. But the family goes to the park and watches them from there. Good view, fewer people."

"How crowded could it possibly be? This is Connelly. What's the population? A thousand cowboys and cowgirls?"

"Why are you here again?"

She leaned forward. "You're grumpy when you wake up. Or should I say grumpier."

"I'm not used to people just walking into my house and..." He stopped talking when Abby came through the front door. He looked at Harper. "She's my sister."

Abby came and sat next to Tanner and patted his knee. "How's the arm?"

"Hurts."

"Did you sleep here?"

"Why does it matter?"

She frowned at him. "Man, you're grumpy today." She stood. "I'll make you some coffee. Harper, do you want some?"

"No thanks. I don't drink it."

Abby stopped walking. "Oh. That's right. Do you have any tea, Tanner?"

"Why would I have tea?"

"I'll just go get that coffee going."

Harper stood. "Okay. I'll get out of your hair. I didn't mean to make you mad again. Are you sure I can borrow a truck?"

"Yes. Please. Borrow a truck."

"Okay. If I see you tonight, I'll turn around and go in the other direction."

"You don't need to do that." She headed for the door, and Tanner sighed. He hated himself for what he was about to say. "Harper."

"Yes?"

"We always gather at the north end of the park. If you want to join us, you're welcome to."

"Thank you. That's very nice of you."

"Just be forewarned. We'll be grilling steaks and drinking beer."

"That's fine. What time do you get there?"

"About seven while everyone else is at the dance."

"I'll see you at seven, then."

"See you then."

When Abby came back in with two cups of coffee, Tanner was lying on the couch again. She set a cup down on the table, then sat in the chair.

"Where's Harper?"

"She went home."

"How?"

"I let her take one of the trucks."

"Oh. Okay." She put her feet on the table and took a sip of coffee. "So, what's going on with you two?"

Tanner sat back up and grabbed his cup of coffee. "Nothing is going on. Except for the fact she won't leave me alone."

"I think she likes you."

"She doesn't like me. You make it sound like we're in high school."

"Well, I like her. She's..."

"Annoying?"

"No. Independent. And she's trying to make it in a field dominated by men. At least around here. Throw in the fact she's young and pretty, and no one wants to take her seriously."

"She's socially inept. And she has definite boundary issues. And by that, I mean not being able to recognize them."

Abby smiled. "Has Harper stepped on your boundary?"

"She's stepped on it, crossed over it, and is completely unaware there ever was one."

"I'm sure you're overreacting."

"I'm not." He took a sip of his coffee.

"Well, it's not like you're going to be seeing her again anytime soon."

He glanced at her over the rim of his cup. "Not until tonight."

"Tonight?"

"I sort of told her she could come to our fireworks barbecue tonight."

Abby smiled. "You did, huh?"

He rested his cup on his knee and leaned back on the cushions. "Only because she's new in town and she doesn't know anyone. No one should have to watch fireworks on the Fourth of July by themselves."

Abby cocked her head. "There's my sweet baby brother. I knew you were still in there somewhere."

After they finished their coffee, Abby went to feed the horses, and Tanner went up to his room to take a shower. He wrapped his cast in a plastic grocery bag, then secured it above his elbow. He looked at it.

"Damn Max." He blamed Max one hundred percent. It wasn't Chester's fault.

Tanner took a long shower. He'd slept pretty well, despite the fact he'd spent the night on the couch. It'd now been three nights since he slept in his bed.

After the shower, he looked at his face in the mirror and ran a hand over his chin. He shaved every couple of weeks. Tobias and Deacon could maintain the couple days' worth of growth look. With their dark hair, it looked good. But Tanner's beard was reddish blond and not very thick. It took him two weeks to get it to where it started looking okay. But then he'd get tired of it and he'd shave it off.

He used to think it was because his hair was so light. But Skyler was blond and his scruffy beard looked good.

Tanner shook his head at his reflection. "You just weren't meant to wear a beard, I guess." But without facial hair, he thought he looked like a kid.

He growled at the mirror. "Who cares? It's not like you're trying to impress anyone." When Harper popped into his mind. He scowled. "Man, don't even. That's a can of worms you don't want to open."

He put on a red shirt in honor of the holiday, then joined Abby in the barn. She was in the pen with Lucy and El Primero.

Tanner leaned on the gate. "How're they doing?"

Abby watched the colt for a moment. "I swear this little guy is growing already."

"Speaking of little guys. Where are yours?"

"Skyler took them to the parade."

Tanner raised an eyebrow. "Alone?"

"Yeah. In the double stroller. He'll be fine."

"You married a brave man."

"I sometimes think he's a better mother than I am."

She came through the gate and Tanner hugged her. "No way. He's a better cook. And he's a better rider. But mother, nah."

"Thanks. He knew what he was getting into as far as the cooking goes."

"That's true."

"And you're one to talk. Ruthie makes all your meals for you."

He shrugged. "What can I say? I'm sweet Tanner."

She walked down to Chester's stall. "Well, sweet Tanner. What are we going to do about Chester here?"

"I need to get him into the pen again."

She looked at him. "Not today. You just broke your arm yesterday."

"Come out with me. We'll work him together."

"Tanner."

He smiled at her. "You know you want to."

"Fine."

She got a handful of oats and held it out to Chester. When he came to eat them, she hooked a lead line on him, then led him out of the pen.

Tanner walked in front of her. "Take it nice and slow. No sudden moves and no loud noises."

"I've worked with skittish horses before, Tanner."

"Yeah, well, this one dumped me off yesterday. So let's be extra cautious."

Abby took Chester to the smaller training pen and lunged him for about twenty minutes while Tanner watched. She talked to Chester quietly and kept him moving. He did well and followed her commands to speed up or slow down. He was much calmer today, probably due to the fact Max wasn't there, and he hadn't just endured a ride in the horse trailer.

When Abby slowed Chester down to a walk, Tanner went into the pen to see what the horse would do when he got close. Chester hesitated for a moment when he saw Tanner, but then walked on by.

Tanner smiled. "Look at you all calm and acting normal." Chester made one more circle, then Tanner held up his hand. "Have him stop, Abby."

Abby said, "Whoa, boy," and gave the lunge line a slight pull. Chester stopped and looked at her.

Tanner approached him. "Hey. Remember me? We were getting along just fine yesterday until Max showed up."

Chester stared at him.

"Are we friends again?" Tanner moved closer and ran a hand down Chester's back. "That's a good boy. No nerves today. Good job."

Abby put her hands on her hips. "Tanner. Do not get up on Chester's back."

He glanced at her. "He's not going to hurt me again."

"No. But I might. Please, give your arm at least one day, before you start riding nervous horses around the pen bareback."

"Fine. How about with a saddle?"

"No. No riding for you today."

Tanner sighed and rubbed Chester's ears. "She can be a bit of a B I T C H, but you'll get used to it."

Skyler came up to the gate. "Did you just call my wife a bitch?"

Tanner turned and looked at him. "No. That wasn't me. It was Chester here. His mouth is out of control."

"Hmm. Okay."

Abby cocked her head. "Where are our daughters?"

"Asleep in the truck."

"You can't leave them alone."

"Hon, they're fifty feet away."

"Still." She left the pen and headed for the truck.

"Don't wake them up. They just fell asleep on the way home." Skyler looked at Tanner, who laughed. Skyler pointed at him. "Don't say it."

Chapter Eleven

"Maybe you can spead the word I'm not a quack or a witch."

Tanner was sitting at a picnic table next to Gemma, who was massaging his fingers. He hadn't asked her to. She'd just taken it upon herself to do it. Gemma was on edge these days, and Tanner did his best to not upset her.

"So, how long will you be in the cast? Six weeks?"

"Something like that."

"Even though it may hurt, keep moving your fingers."

"Yeah, okay." He winced at what she was doing.

"Sorry."

Tobias walked over and sat next to her. "Leave the poor kid alone, Gem. He just broke it yesterday."

Gemma patted Tanner's hand and stopped what she was doing. "Fine. I just want him to have a complete recovery."

"He's young. He'll bounce right back." He handed Tanner a beer. "Drink up."

Gemma looked at Tanner. "Are you taking pain medication?"

"Um..."

Tobias nudged Gemma. "Leave the kid alone."

She kissed Tobias on the cheek. "Fine. I guess he took care of you plenty of times while you were self-medicating." She got up and walked away.

Tanner glanced at Tobias. "Are you two okay?"

"Oh yeah. She's sleep deprived. And has been nauseous for three months, which means she basically hasn't eaten in three months. She'll be back in a minute."

A few minutes later, Gemma returned and sat down on Tobias' lap. "I'm sorry."

He kissed her. "I know you are. And it's fine because I love you and I know you love me."

She looked at Tanner. "I'm sorry. You don't need me mother-henning you."

Tanner smiled. "It's okay. For all the same reasons Tobias said. Except for loving you. I mean I do. But not like he does. But you knew that."

Tobias patted him on the shoulder. "Stop talking, Tanner."

"Right." He took a sip of his beer.

Everyone was there, the whole family. All the kids. But so far, Harper hadn't showed up. It was fine, though. Tanner didn't care if she showed or not. In fact, he preferred she didn't.

Tobias nudged him. "So where's your friend?"

"She's hardly a friend."

"Okay. Where's the person you spent most of the last two days with?"

Tanner shrugged. "Maybe she's not coming."

Gemma put her arms around Tobias' neck. "Now you leave him alone."

"Me? I'm just asking a question."

Riley ran up to them. "Dad, will you come play monster freeze tag with us?"

"Sure." He glanced at Tanner. "Do you feel up to a game of monster freeze tag?"

Tanner smiled. "Sure." He drank some more beer, then set his bottle on the table.

Gemma started to say something, but Tobias pointed at her, then kissed her. "He'll be okay."

She looked at Riley. "Make sure the kids take it easy on Uncle Tanner's arm."

"Sure, Mom. We know."

"Thank you, honey." She stood, and Tobias got to his feet and put a hand on Riley's back.

"Let's go freeze some kids."

Tanner followed Tobias and Riley to the open grass, where the other kids were running around. There were six of them, including Deacon's three oldest girls, and Tobias' three boys.

Gemma sat at the picnic table and watched them. After a few minutes, Cassidy joined her with baby Luna, as the kids screamed in delight while running from the two monsters, Tobias and Tanner.

Abby came to the table, holding Gianna. Gemma smiled at her and touched her hand. "Hi there, Gianna. Pretty soon, you and your sister will be right out there with your silly cousins and your crazy uncles."

Abby watched them for a moment. "Should Tanner be out there running around like that?"

"I tried to stop him, but Tobias gave me the look."

"Oh yeah. Tobias is all about doing what you shouldn't. How's the morning sickness going? Any better?"

"It's should be called morning, afternoon, and evening sickness. Still going strong. I can't keep much down, so I'm not gaining any weight. Dr. Hart isn't too thrilled about it. But he hasn't given me a solution yet, either."

"I felt sorry for myself when I had it for a month. And you're right. Dr. Hart's advice is eating some crackers before you get up."

Gemma raised her hand. "Going on three months now."

Cassidy patted her knee. "It has to end soon."

"That's what everyone keeps telling me. I guess I'll eventually have the baby. It's bound to end then."

When Tanner slipped on the wet grass and fell onto one knee, all three women got to their feet.

Tobias jogged to him and helped him up. "I'm good." Tanner waved at the women. "Just wet grass."

As they sat back down, Harper approached the table. "Hi."

Abby smiled at her. "Hey, hi. I'm glad you came. Do you know everyone?"

"Um..." She smiled at Gemma. "I haven't met you yet. You must be Tobias' wife."

Gemma stood and shook hands with her. "Yes. I'm Gemma." Tobias ran by chasing after Thea. "I'm married to crazy Tobias."

Gemma watched Harper take in the kids playing tag and Deacon with Skyler, holding Gillian at the barbecue. "There are a lot of us."

"Yes. It's quite the family."

"Well, we're very fortunate all the kids are growing up with their cousins and aunts and uncles."

"It's great. My brother and I had one set of grandparents we saw at Christmas."

Cassidy raised a hand. "No brother. But I had a wonderful grandfather who I spent every summer with."

"Tanner told me he's living on your grandfather's ranch."

"Yes. Which I'm very thankful for. I'm glad we were able to incorporate it into the Starlight. Grandpa would be so proud of what Abby, Skyler, and Tanner have built there."

Harper nodded. "It's quite the operation." She watched Tanner for a moment. "Should he be out there playing like that the day after breaking his arm?"

Gemma laughed. "Have a seat, Harper. I like you."

The game ended, and Tanner returned to the table when he spotted Harper.

He gave her a nod. "Hey."

"Hi."

He picked up his beer and took a long drink. Gemma glanced at him, then called all the kids to come to the table.

"Okay, you guys. I want to introduce you to Harper. She's the new vet in town, and she's joining us for the barbecue and the fireworks show." She glanced at Harper. "We don't expect you to remember all their names." The kids were lined up in front of them. "So, the boys are all mine. Riley, Grady, and Jordan. The girls are Cassidy's. Thea, Emery, and Kinsley. Then we have baby Luna. And Abby's twins, Gianna and Gillian, over there with her dad."

"Wow. I'll never remember your names. Not at first, anyway. But it's nice to meet you all."

Gemma waved at the kids. "Okay. You can go now." They ran off, and Tobias came to retrieve his beer.

"Glad you could make it, Harper."

"Thank you. How's Chance doing?"

"Much better. Seems your herbs are doing the trick."

"I'm so glad to hear that. Maybe you can spread the word I'm not a quack or a witch."

"I'm sure that's not what people think. Not yet anyway. You haven't been here long enough for them to form an opinion."

"I guess I'd like to put it out there before they get a chance to think it."

Gemma smiled. "Well, I think it's great. I don't suppose you have any magical potion to deal with morning sickness?"

Harper thought for a moment. "Actually, I just might."

"Oh my gosh. Really?"

"Yes. No guarantee. But I'll do some research tonight and mix you up something."

"I would be eternally grateful."

Tobias grinned. "Mixing secret potions? You really are a witch. But my wife isn't a horse. And obviously, she is pregnant, so..."

"I won't give her anything that would hurt the baby. You can even run it by the doctor before you take it. In fact, I recommend you do. And as for her not being a horse. Well, herbal medicine is for everyone. Human or otherwise."

Gemma looked at Tobias. "If the doctor says it's okay. I'm going to try anything if it has a chance of calming down my stomach."

Tobias nodded. "Okay. I understand. I didn't mean any offense, Harper."

"None taken. I'm quite used to being questioned."

Tobias looked at Tanner, who raised an eyebrow and nodded. "I'm gonna go check and see how the steaks are coming along."

He made his escape, and Gemma smiled at Harper. "Excuse my husband. He worries about me."

"It's not a problem. Really. I get it. He loves you."

———————⬧———————

When Tanner realized he was at the table with all the women, he took his beer and went to join his brothers.

Tobias glanced back at Harper. "I didn't mean to insult her."

Tanner shook his head. "I don't think it's even possible to insult her. She doesn't seem to get subtleties like that."

Deacon laughed. "What are you talking about?"

"She's kind of in her own world."

"She's super smart, right?"

"Yeah. I guess. How do you know that?"

"Dr. Benton talked to me about her before he hired her. Graduated vet school at twenty-two."

"He talked to you about her?"

"Yeah. He was a little concerned her non-traditional way of thinking would be a hard-sell around here."

Tobias laughed. "He wasn't wrong."

"Well, we need to make sure she gets the respect she deserves and has a fighting chance around here."

Tobias looked at Harper. "Respect?"

"Why do you have a problem with her?"

Tobias put a hand on Tanner's shoulder. "Our little brother is infatuated with the young doctor."

Tanner stepped away from Tobias. "What the hell? I am not. Shit. She's done nothing but hang around and annoy me."

Skyler laughed. "Yeah, I bet she was super annoying spending the night with you in the barn."

"Shut up. I'm going to go sit with the kids."

He left his brothers and went to Riley, who was sitting in the grass by himself. Tanner knelt next to him. "Why aren't you out there with the rest of the kids?"

'They're playing a stupid kid game. "

"Oh. Yeah. I guess it's tough being the oldest brother and cousin."

"Sometimes."

"I had the opposite problem, being the youngest. You get to choose to stay out of something. I got left out of everything, whether I wanted to be or not."

"That's kind of rough."

Tanner nodded. "Maybe. But I showed them. I spent a lot of time talking to the horses and the other animals."

Riley grinned. "And now you're the horse whisperer."

"Damn right."

"Can you teach me how to do that? I think it's really cool."

"Well, I don't know exactly how it works. But if you want to start hanging around a bit more. I'll gladly show you what works for me."

"Yeah. Cool. I'd love that."

"Alright. I'll talk to Tobias and see if we can get you to the horse ranch a few times a week."

In the seven years since Riley and Gemma came to live on the Starlight Ranch, he'd become quite an accomplished rider. He'd been asking Tobias and Gemma if he could start training for some equestrian events, and they told him he could once he turned fifteen. With Tobias' and Skyler's help, he had a chance of being really good. And everyone in the family agreed equestrian riding was a safer bet than rodeo.

At this point, Tanner was the only Carmichael still competing in oc-casional rodeo events. Abby had stopped once she got pregnant with the twins. All the adult Carmichaels, along with Skyler, still competed and generally won the chasing of the hounds event every year during Gala weekend. But for the last several years, they formed two teams. The women against the men. It was a toss-up every year as to which team won.

Chapter Twelve

"Would you really tackle a pregnant woman?"

Tobias and Deacon dragged three picnic tables over and lined them up to make one long table. When everyone sat down, Tanner sat next to Harper. Gemma was on Harper's other side, and Tanner had Thea next to him. She loved her Uncle Tobias. But Tanner was her favorite uncle.

Tanner looked around the table of food. There was a lot of it. But most of it, Harper wouldn't eat. He glanced at her.

"Sorry, there's not much here for you to eat."

"It's fine. I'll have some salad and the peas look good."

Gemma smiled. "They're from my garden. Completely organic."

"Perfect."

Cassidy was sitting across from them and offered her a slice of bread. "No eggs. No animal fat."

Harper smiled. "Thank you. I appreciate you understanding."

Cassidy leaned across the table and lowered her voice. "I dated a vegan guy. It's so restrictive. You must be very dedicated."

"It's the only thing I've ever known, so I'm used to it."

Tobias sat next to Gemma before looking around her at Harper. "This is fresh Carmichael beef. You don't know what you're missing."

"I think I do. But please enjoy." She put some salad on her plate, then turned to Tanner. "How fresh is fresh?"

"It was probably butchered yesterday."

Harper turned a little green. "Wow." She stuck her fork in a piece of lettuce.

"That lettuce is even fresher. Probably plucked out of the garden this morning. Poor lettuce. Just trying to live its life. Not bothering anyone."

Harper threw an elbow into his side, and Tanner laughed.

Gemma stared at her empty plate, and Tobias put his arm around her. "Nothing looks good?"

"It all looks good. I just know as soon as I eat it, it's going to come right back up." She looked at Harper. "What here would be easiest on my stomach?"

"A little salad. Chew it well and avoid the onions. The fruit salad. Jello is always good on an unsettled stomach. And maybe a little bread."

"Okay. I'll give it a try."

Thea nudged Tanner. "Will you cut my meet for me, please?"

"Sure." He cut up her small piece of steak, then glanced at Harper, who was watching him. "What?"

"Nothing."

"Hmm."

Cassidy smiled. "Tanner?"

"Yeah."

"How's El Primero doing?"

"He's great. We sent his picture to the clients on our waiting list. They all want him."

"That's great. How do you decide who gets him?"

"The guy at the top of the list. As long as he comes through with the money. We need to get a couple more mares and breed them. We can sell every damn foal we produce."

"Deacon said as much the other day."

Deacon came up behind Cassidy and sat between her and Emery. "What did I say the other day?"

"That we need to purchase a few more mares."

"Definitely. We're on our way."

Tanner set his fork down. "I hope some of them stay around long enough for me to work with them."

"I'm sure training will become part of the whole package. If you're going to spend that kind of money on a horse, you might as well have it trained by the best damn trainers in the country."

Emery nudged him. "Daddy. Bad word."

"Sorry, honey."

Harper joined the conversation. "How many mares can your stallion service?"

"More mares than we're ever likely to have." Deacon smiled at her. "We want to keep it in the family. So we don't want to produce more horses than Tanner, Skyler, and Abby can handle. We think hands on produces the best quality."

"They don't have any hired help?"

Tanner spoke up. "We have a small staff who helps with feeding, grooming, and cleaning stalls. Once in a while, they'll do some riding. But we like to handle most the exercising and training ourselves. We're going for quality personal care, over churning out a bunch of inadequately trained horses."

She nodded. "I like that. You can afford to pay to have it all done. But you prefer to do it yourself. Very commendable."

"We don't do it to be commended. We do it because we love it. And what's the point of paying someone else to do it for you?"

Deacon cocked his head at Tanner. "She wasn't attacking you, Tanner. She was admiring our way of doing things."

Tanner took a breath. "Yeah. I know."

Harper glanced at Tanner, then smiled at Deacon. "I'm afraid your brother doesn't know quite what to think of me. I've been a bit of a nuisance for the last couple of days."

Tanner stopped himself from saying, 'a bit'? Instead, he took another bite of steak.

By the time everyone was done eating dinner, followed by various desserts, the sun was going down. The fireworks would begin in an hour and a half. It was time for the Carmichael Fourth of July flag football game. It took some convincing to get Harper to join the women's team, but she finally agreed, making it clear she had no idea what she was doing.

Gemma wanted to play, too, despite not feeling well. So, Deacon made an announcement before the game started.

"We each have a handicapped player. Gemma and Tanner. So, take it easy on them. If someone needs to tap out, Riley will be the alternate player." He looked at Tanner. "Before we start, give Harper the basic rules of the game."

Tanner walked over to Harper. "Everyone wears two flags on either side. Instead of tackling, all you have to do is grab your opponent's flag. If the guy or girl with the ball loses their flag, it stops the play. No tackling, diving, or blocking. The ball can only be thrown forward. If you catch the ball, run like hell for the goal line and try to avoid losing a flag. That's about it. You'll pick it up quick enough."

"So. No rough play. No one gets hurt."

"Um...sure."

"That sounds real affirmative."

"Watch out for Tobias. He gets carried away. And Abby. She's crazy competitive. But she's on your team, so you shouldn't have to worry about her."

"Okay, I guess I got it."

"You'll be fine. Just...chill and try to have some fun."

"I'm chill."

Deacon was quarterback on the men's team, and Abby was the women's team quarterback. As always happened, the game escalated quickly from playful teasing to badgering, and everything just short of cheating. Tobias and Abby had it out for each other, and Deacon took on the role of peacekeeper and impartial referee. Tanner tried to stay out of most of the crazy plays, as did Gemma. Harper was just trying to keep on top of what was happening and who had the ball.

When she found herself to be the only one open and Abby tossed her the ball, she was as shocked as everyone else when she caught it. She made a dash for the goal line, which was between two trees.

Tanner went charging after her. The last thing he wanted was for her to be able to brag about making the one and only goal. When Harper was ten feet from the trees, Tanner lunged and threw himself through the air, realizing, while in mid-flight, he was probably going to hurt himself when he landed.

He tackled Harper to the ground and landed on top of her as the ball flew out of her hands. He took a moment to realize what had happened, then smiled at her.

"Whoops."

She pushed him off and he rolled onto his back. "Whoops? You tackled me."

He sat up and hugged his knees. "You were headed for the goal line."

She sat and glared at him. "You tackled me. You broke the rules."

He laughed. "Sorry. I lost my head."

The rest of them had now gathered around.

Tobias grinned. "Good job, man."

Harper looked at Tobias. "He tackled me."

Tanner reached over and pulled off one of her flags. "Now you're tackled."

Abby, being competitive Abby, picked up the abandoned ball and headed for the goal line. Skyler took off after her and caught her before she crossed. He grabbed her and wrestled her to the ground. Abby dropped the ball as she embraced Skyler and kissed him. Gemma ran to pick it up, then pointed at Tobias and Deacon.

"Would you really tackle a pregnant woman?" She walked the ball across the goal line, then performed a victory dance.

Tobias laughed. "Man, you women are cheaters. Making out with the opposing team. Using the pregnancy excuse."

Tanner looked at Harper. "Are you okay?"

"Yes." She smiled. "I can't believe you tackled me. Is your arm okay?"

He moved his arm. "Yeah. Doesn't hurt any more than it already did. Although my leg hurts a bit."

"Serves you right. I was about to make my first ever goal."

"Sorry. Maybe next time."

"How often do you do this?"

"We try to limit it to once a year. Although we have been known to have a Thanksgiving Bowl, weather permitting."

"I think you Carmichaels are a bit crazy."

"You could be right."

She got to her feet, then looked down at him. "Do you need some help, old man?"

"I'm two years older than you."

She held out her hand, and Tanner grabbed it with his right hand and let her pull him to his feet. The leg he hurt when he fell off Chester hurt again. But just like then, he knew it was something that would go away pretty quick. He went to the ice chest and took out a beer. Harper had followed him, and he handed her a bottle of water.

"I need to walk off this injury. Care to take a stroll to the gazebo?"

"Sure."

They headed across the grass, and Tanner glanced at her. "You did pretty good, seeing as it was your first time and all."

"I was doing fine until you tackled me."

"Keep complaining. I don't care. Because, honestly, it was worth it."

She stop walking and looked at him. "Do you enjoy tackling defenseless women?"

"No. Just you. And I'm pretty sure you're a long way from being defenseless."

"You're right. I am. So don't you forget it."

"You'd never let me."

They arrived at the gazebo and sat on the bench running around the inside edge of the structure.

Tanner took a sip of his beer. "I'm glad you came tonight."

"You are?"

"Yeah. Why wouldn't I be?"

She shrugged. "Because I'm pretty sure you invited me to be polite. And you never thought I'd show up."

"You think you know me so well?"

"I know enough."

"You don't know me." He drank some more beer.

She glanced at him. "I know animals and kids love you. So, that's a good sign. And even though you're the baby brother, your family respects you and your talent with horses. They know you're an important and valuable asset to the business."

"If you know all that in three days, then you've been hanging around too much."

She laughed. "Well, we both know that's true."

They heard the explosion of a firework and looked toward the sound.

"It's starting." Harper looked at Tanner. "Should we go join the others?"

"No. This is the best seat in the house."

As the sky continued to light up in a vibrant display of colors, Riley, Thea, Emery, and Grady came running across the grass.

Riley called out. "Can we watch with you, Uncle Tanner?"

"Of course. Hurry up. You don't want to miss it." He picked Emery up and put her on his shoulders, and the six of them watched the show.

Harper leaned in toward Tanner. "Kids and animals."

"Well, good thing I love them back."

Chapter Thirteen

"I told you they were idiots."

Tanner was riding Lucy around the arena. She was a magnificent horse and he could've ridden her all day. He'd been at it for thirty minutes when his phone rang. He thought about ignoring it, but it could be a business call, so he should at least look at the number.

He slowed Lucy to a walk, then sighed when he saw the call was from Harper. It'd been four days since the Fourth and he hadn't seen her since. He hated to admit it, but he'd been wondering what she was up to. He answered the call.

"Dr. Waverly."

"Tanner."

He could tell by the sound of her voice something wasn't right. "What's wrong?"

"I'm kind of cornered in a stall by a horse that isn't very happy with the fact I'm here."

"Cornered?"

"Yes. He's blocking me from leaving. Every time I move, he snorts and stomps his foot."

Tanner trotted Lucy to the arena entrance. "Where are you at?"

"Burt Carson's place."

"Stay put. Don't try to get out. I'll be there in fifteen minutes."

He stashed his phone and dismounted, then led Lucy out of the arena. He spotted one of the men and called to him. "Jack! Come take Lucy."

"What's up, boss?"

"I've got to go help someone. Can you cool her down and put her away?"

"Sure thing."

Tanner handed the horse off to Jack, then ran for his truck.

Abby was coming out of the barn. "Where are you off to so fast?"

"Harper is stuck in a stall with an ornery horse over at Burt Carson's place."

"Do you need help?"

"No. I should be able to handle it. I'll call you if I do."

He jumped into the truck and sped off. Burt was the retired postmaster and his place was only thirty acres with a house and a barn. He had four horses he kept around for his grandchildren to ride, which were gentle and not the type of horse that would hold someone hostage in the stall. Tanner wasn't quite sure what he'd find when he got there.

He arrived at the property and parked next to Harper's truck, then went inside. Just as she'd said, Harper was in the back of a stall, with a big black horse blocking her from the gate. The horse wasn't one of Burt's. Tanner looked around for some oats, then put some in a bucket. He shook it as he approached the stall.

"Hey you big black bastard. Look what I have for you." The horse continued to stare at Harper. Tanner shook the can again. "I know you want this. Yum, yum."

The horse glanced back at Tanner, gave Harper one more evil glare, then turned and headed for the bucket. Tanner moved down the side of the stall to draw the horse away from the gate. He kept eye contact with the horse. "Harper, start walking toward the gate. Stick to the far side. Move slow and try not to make any noise."

She nodded and started doing what he said.

The horse stuck his nose into the bucket. "Okay. Keep going. You can speed up. He's pretty invested in the oats."

Harper made it to the gate. When she opened it, the horse lifted his head and looked at her. Tanner shook the bucket again, and the horse resumed eating. Harper stepped out of the stall and closed the gate, then moved to the center of the barn.

Tanner glanced at her. "Are you okay?" When she didn't answer him, he poured the rest of the oats out in the stall, and went to her. "Harper?"

She was trembling, and she looked at him with tears in her eyes. He held his arms out, and she fell into them. He hugged her and rubbed her back as she laid her head against his chest.

"You're okay. Everything's okay."

She nodded, but stayed in his embrace. Finally, after a few minutes, the shaking subsided, and she stepped away from him and whispered. "Sorry."

"You've got nothing to be sorry for." He took her arm. "Come sit down." He led her to a bail of straw and sat her down. There was an old refrigerator, and he opened it and found a bottle of water. He brought it to her before sitting down next to her.

She drank some water. "I was sure he was going to stomp me."

"What happened? Burt's horses have always been gentle. His grandkids ride them."

"This is a new horse. He just got it. For a good price, he said. I wonder why?"

"How'd you end up in the stall?"

She took another sip of water. "Burt asked me to come check him out."

"Wait. Burt called you and asked you to come check out the horse?"

"Yeah. Why?"

"Burt's in Ohio at his niece's wedding." Tanner got up and looked at the horse. Upon closer inspection, he saw the small brand on the horse's rump.

"Damn Conner brothers."

"Who?" Harper stood and walked toward Tanner, but didn't want to get too close to the stall.

"Let me see your phone and the call from Burt."

She pulled up her call log and handed him the phone. Tanner took out his phone and dialed the number. When a familiar voice answered, he hung up. "Bastards."

"What's going on?"

He handed the phone back to Harper. "You've been played by a couple of assholes."

"Why would they set me up like this?"

"I'm sure they thought they'd have some fun with the new vet. The new young female vet."

"I could've been killed."

"Yeah. I'm sure that wasn't their intention, but they're not very bright." He took out his phone again and called Skyler.

"What's up? Abby said you took off like a bat out of hell."

"The Conner brothers left a little surprise, in the form of a big black ornery horse, for Harper over at Burt's place."

"Isn't Burt in Ohio?"

"Yep. But she didn't know that. Can you bring a trailer over here?"

"To Burt's, sure. What are you thinking?"

"I'm thinking we just got ourselves a new horse to work with." He went to the stall and looked at the horse. "He's pretty good looking. Just needs to be put in his place."

"Tanner Carmichael. Are you talking about stealing a horse?"

"No. I'm rescuing a poor horse I found abandoned on the property. If they want to come get it. They're free to do so."

"I'll be right there."

Harper folded her arms across her chest. "What are you doing?"

"The Conners are a family full of bastards. Dad and two sons. They don't have the first clue how to treat an animal. They brand their horses, which is barbaric. And they think it's hilarious to set up the new vet with a dangerous animal."

"Alright. They're bastards."

"So, instead of going over there and kicking their asses, I'm going to take their horse."

"Aren't they going to want it back?"

"I'm pretty sure they're at least smart enough to know what they did is a criminal act. I don't expect they'll come by. But if they do. They'll need to go through me, my brothers, and Skyler, before they get their horse back."

Harper put a hand to her mouth. "You're doing this for me?"

"Yes. And because that horse is just as much a victim as you are."

Harper went to him and hugged him again. "Thank you."

"You're welcome."

She stepped back. "No one has ever stood up for me."

"We can't have people treating our new vet like this."

She nodded. "Were they trying to scare me off?"

"Probably. Jokes on them, right?"

She laughed. "Damn right."

Skyler walked into the barn twenty minutes later and went to Harper. "Are you okay?"

She nodded. "Yes. Thanks to Tanner."

He walked over to the stall. "Pretty good-looking horse."

Tanner smiled. "Yeah, when he's not snorting and stomping at you." He turned to Harper. "You can go get in the truck if you want. I'm not sure how much trouble he's going to give us when we put him in the trailer."

"I'd kind of like to see this." She closed herself into an empty stall. "I'll watch from here."

Tanner grinned. "Okay." He filled the grain bucket again, then held it out to Skyler.

Skyler shook his head. "You've only got one good arm. I'll lead him out of here. You man the bucket."

"Okay. He does like the oats." Tanner held the bucket for the horse again and when he came to eat, Skyler hooked a lead line to his halter.

"Come on you bastard. Let's get you into the trailer." Skyler opened the gate and Tanner moved in front of it with the bucket. The horse came calmly out of the stall and followed Tanner as he walked out of the barn and headed for the trailer.

Harper came out of the stall she was in and followed them. "Why's he being so calm now?"

Tanner shook his head. "Who knows?"

Skyler led him into the trailer and secured him, then came out with a grin. "Nothing to it."

Harper shook her head. "He really did try to kill me."

He laughed. "I believe you." As he closed the rear of the trailer, a pickup pulled into the drive and parked by the house. Eric and Ray Conner got out and approached the horse trailer.

"Hey. That's our horse."

Tanner glanced at Harper. "I told you they were idiots."

Skyler took a few steps toward the men. "You mean the horse that tried to kill Dr. Waverly?"

The brothers exchanged a glance. "We don't know anything about that. We just came to get our horse."

"Why is your horse here at Burt's place? He's out of town. We weren't going to call the sheriff, but when you call to report we stole your horse, I guess we can add trespassing to the attempted murder charge."

Eric, the older of the two, took a step back. "Keep the bastard. He was headed to the glue factory next week anyway."

When Tanner took a step forward, Harper put a hand on his arm. "They're really not worth it."

Tanner took a breath and relaxed. "You're right."

The Conners headed for their truck and Skyler called out after them. "The next time you try something like this, you'll lose a lot more than your damn horse."

They got into their truck and peeled out.

Skyler turned back to Tanner and shrugged. "Sorry. Didn't mean to steal your thunder."

"No worries. I know you and the Conners go way back."

"Yep. Back to high school. Thought they could pick on the rich kid."

Tanner glanced at Harper. "Skyler was an only child. He didn't have two big brothers to look out for him." He smiled at Skyler. "As I recall, one of them ended up with a broken arm."

Harper laughed. "Sounds like he got off easy."

Chapter Fourteen

"I thought we weren't being you and me today."

No one else tried so blatantly to get rid of Harper, as the Conner brothers did. They just didn't call her at all. Either the ranches surrounding Connelly were having an exceptional run of good luck with healthy animals, or Harper was getting the cold shoulder. She was pretty sure it was the latter.

She refused to get discouraged, though. They'd come around when an emergency happened or they got tired of driving to Taylorville to visit the vet there. The only problem was, she was running out of money. Between the rent on the clinic and the rent on her house, she had about run through her savings. Something had to happen fast, or Connelly would find itself without a vet and she'd be living in her brother's spare room back in Austin.

She was at the coffee shop, sipping some orange juice and contemplating her plight when Tanner walked by. She hoped he'd keep going, but he spotted her and gave her a wave. She waved back. *Just keep moving, cowboy. I'm too depressed to talk to you right now.*

Tanner changed directions and came through the door. He removed his hat and ran a hand through his hair as he walked to her table. "Good morning,"

"Is it?"

He pulled out the chair across from her and sat down, then set his hat on the empty chair next to him. "Uh oh. What's up?"

"Nothing. Why'd you come in? I thought you'd be glad to be rid of me for a few days."

"I couldn't let you sit here by yourself. It's pretty pathetic."

"Wow. Thanks. Maybe I want to sit her by myself. Maybe I enjoy my own company."

Tanner slid his chair back and picked up his hat. "Fine. I'll leave you to it."

Harper reached for his arm. "No. Please stay. I'm sorry. I am pathetic." She really didn't want to be alone now that he was here.

He set his hat back down. "No, you're not. I was kidding. Mostly."

She looked at him for a moment. "Can we not be me and you for a few minutes? I just don't have it in me today."

"Sure. Have you eaten?"

"I was sitting here trying to figure out what I could get for five dollars. I already splurged on orange juice. Can you believe this little glass of orange juice is four dollars? Of course, you never need to worry about how expensive things are. You're Tanner Carmichael."

Tanner slid the menu in front of her. "Order whatever you want. On me."

"I wasn't trying to—"

"I know. Find some non-animal related food items on there and order."

She opened the menu. "Are you going to eat?"

"Already did. Sunday is family breakfast day."

"Of course it is." She cocked her head. "Your family can't possibly be as perfect as it appears to be."

Tanner laughed. "We're not perfect. We have Tobias."

Harper raised an eyebrow. "I actually like Tobias."

"Well sure. Everyone does."

"But?"

"No buts."

She set the menu down in front of her. "You can't sit here and watch me eat. That'd just be weird."

"Fine. I'll have a coffee." He waved at the waitress, who came over with a smile.

"Hi Tanner."

He nodded. "Hester."

Harper did a double take at the woman, who looked extremely familiar.

Tanner smiled. "This is Hester, Hallie's twin sister."

"Oh, okay." *Identical twins. Interesting.* "Hi. I'm Harper."

Hester nodded. "The new vet. I heard about you." She turned her attention to Tanner. "Coffee this morning?"

Harper could tell she was being flirtatious, but Tanner didn't seem to be picking up on it.

"Yes, please."

"How's the horse business coming along? I heard you got yourselves a couple of really fancy horses."

"Yeah. Branching out a little."

"Cool." She glanced at Harper and her smile faded. "Are you ready to order?"

"I'm going to need another minute."

"Okay. I'll be back." She put a hand on Tanner's arm. "Nice to see you."

"You too, Hester." He watched her walk away, then looked at Harper, who was smiling at him. "What?"

"Hallie and Hester?"

"What about them?"

"Did you date both of them in high school?"

He scowled. "No. Of course not."

"So she just wishes she could ravage you."

"Excuse me?"

Harper touched his arm and took on Hester's tone. "Nice to see you."

"Shut up."

She laughed, then took a breath. "I didn't feel much like laughing today, but then you showed up and here I am, laughing and smiling."

"At my expense."

"Which makes it even better."

"I thought we weren't being you and me today."

"We're not." She picked up the menu and looked at it for several minutes.

Finally, Tanner reached across the table and put his finger on top of it and pulled it down. "I thought maybe you fell asleep back there."

"I'm ready to order."

Tanner waved at Hester again, and a few moments later, she came to the table.

Harper smiled at her. "I'll have the avocado toast with black beans and grilled mushrooms, please."

"Okay." Hester looked at Tanner. "How about you?"

"Just coffee."

"Of course, it's Sunday." She took the menu and wandered off, and Harper shook her head.

"Does everyone in town know it's family breakfast day?"

"Not everyone." He drank some coffee. "So, why were you sitting here like your dog just died?"

"I'm a vet. That's a really bad analogy to use."

Tanner sighed. "Okay. Like... I can't think of another one."

"It'll sound like I'm complaining." She'd love to unburden herself to him. But she wouldn't. They weren't that kind of friends. They weren't even friends, really. Even though he saved her from a crazy horse. And Invited her to his family Fourth of July barbecue. Where he illegally tackled her to the ground and was in no hurry to get off of her.

"Spill. What's going on?"

Maybe she could share a little of what was bothering her. He asked, after all. "Nothing is going on. That's the problem. I've been here for three weeks. Two of them on my own. And I've seen three dogs, a calf, and two horses. One of which was the one who tried to kill me."

"Well, last weekend was the holiday weekend."

"Animals don't time their health issues around human holidays."

Tanner laughed. "I guess not. You're just going to have to be patient. Dr. Benton was here for like a hundred years."

"I understand that. I get that I'm the new kid who doesn't do things the same way as their beloved Dr. Benton. And I have no problem being patient. But I'm pretty sure my two landlords are going to expect me to keep paying the rent." *Why'd I say that? Now he will think I'm pathetic.*

"Shit. I'm sorry. I didn't know it was that bad."

"It's not your problem. And I really hate myself right now for telling you that."

"Harper. Do you want to stick it out and make a go of it? Do you like it here? Is this where you want to stay?"

She answered each of his questions in succession. "Yes. Mostly. I think so."

Tanner grinned. "Then let me help you out."

"How. And why would you want to? You don't even like me." *That's correct, right? You don't like me. Even though I wouldn't mind at all if you did.*

"Who says I don't like you?"

"Um...you. You haven't said the words. But you've made it pretty clear."

He leaned back in his chair and folded his arms across his chest. "I wouldn't be sitting here with you if I didn't like you. A little...tiny...bit."

She smiled. "Fine. Don't worry. I won't tell anyone."

"Good. It'd ruin my street cred."

"You have street cred?"

"Of course. I'm a Carmichael."

"Oh. Right. So, how can you help me?"

"I can keep your rent paid for a few months."

She leaned forward in her chair. "Oh my gosh, no. I couldn't accept that. No."

"We'll consider it a loan. You can pay me back when you're rolling in dough in a few months."

"I don't think I'll ever be rolling in dough. This is Connelly, after all."

"The heart of the Texas Ten."

"Texas Ten?"

"The top ten ranches in northern Texas are spread between here and Amarillo."

"And where does the Starlight Ranch fit on that list?"

"Number one, of course. The Fremont Ranch, Skyler's family ranch, is a distant number two."

"Wow. I had no idea I was sharing a table with the cream of the crop."

"Damn right. You should feel honored." He laughed. "I'm kidding, of course. Not about being number one. But the cocky bastard part."

Hester approached the table with Harper's meal. She set it down, then smiled at Tanner again before leaving the table. Tanner shook his head at the avocado toast.

"My God. That looks disgusting."

"I could say the same thing about your fresh Carmichael steaks at the barbecue." She cut a bite off with her fork and held it out to him. "I dare you to try it."

"I'll try that when you try a bite of steak."

"Never going to happen."

"Likewise."

She ate the bite. "Mmm. Really good."

"Doesn't a human need protein to survive?"

"Black beans. Very high in protein. This has pretty much every food group covered. Except for dairy, of course. And fruit." She held up her juice and took a drink. "Thus the orange juice."

"So about me helping you out?"

"I appreciate the offer. But I need to at least try to figure this out on my own."

"Okay. I can respect that. The offer stands, though."

"Thank you." *You sweet, sweet man.* "And by the way. You're about as far away from a cocky bastard as anyone I've ever met. You try your hardest to get there sometimes. But the ingrained boy scout is too strong."

"Boy scout?"

"Yes."

"Deacon has always been considered the boy scout of the family."

She shook her head. "I don't know Deacon that well yet. And I definitely get the 'be prepared' vibe from him. But you are a true boy scout."

"I'm not sure if you're insulting me or complimenting me."

"It's a compliment. There aren't many gentlemen left in this world. At least from what I've seen."

"Hmm. Well, then thank you. I guess."

"You're welcome." She ate a couple of bites of her meal, then looked at Tanner. "I think we can go back to being you and me now. I'm feeling much better."

"I guess avocado toast with all that crap on it will do that."

Chapter Fifteen

"At least one of us made the jump."

Tanner was watching Lucy and El Primero in the small pasture near the barn. He like to get them out of the stall for a few hours every day for some exercise. The colt was running around and acting crazy, which seemed to be annoying Lucy. He'd zoom past her and she'd whinny at him and act like she was going to nip him. But she wouldn't. It was the human equivalent of 'don't make me count to ten.'

This late in the summer, they often had to water the pasture to keep the grass green. It had been watered earlier in the day, and Primo was getting dirty with his shenanigans.

Tanner laughed at the colt. "You're going to need a bath after this. Which you probably won't appreciate."

Skyler came up beside him. "What's going on out there?"

"Primo is annoying the hell out of his mother."

"Sounds about right."

Tanner glanced at Skyler. "Do you think we could move up our vaccine schedule a little?"

"We don't have a lot of leeway, but a week or so should be fine. Why?"

"Harper could use some business."

"I'll have Abby check the records. We should be able to keep her pretty busy next week."

"Cool. Thanks."

"Is she struggling?"

"Most everyone in town is giving her the cold shoulder. Might help if word gets out we trust her with our horses."

"Sure. Yeah." Skyler nudge Tanner. "So, brother-n-law to brother-in-law, what's going on between you two?"

Tanner glanced at him. "Nothing." At Skyler's raised eyebrow, he added, "Really. We're friends I guess. She doesn't deserve to be boycotted just because she's different from Dr. Benton."

"You're right. She doesn't. But there's something more than that, right? Come on. You can tell me. I won't run off and tell Abby."

Tanner took a moment to answer. He wasn't sure how he felt. There was something about her aside from the annoying part. He took a breath. "I don't know. I don't know how I feel about her."

"Okay. That's honest. This kind of stuff sneaks up on you when you least expect it to."

"I don't want to like her. She drives me crazy. But I think I do."

Skyler smiled and patted him on the back. "Don't be afraid of your feelings, man."

"You've met her, right?"

He grinned. "She's a handful alright. But nothing you can't handle."

"You're giving me way too much credit."

Tanner spent the week working with Chester and a new jumper they got in who was suddenly refusing to jump. He was making some progress with Chester and had started desensitizing him to loud noises. The real test would come, though, when Max came by in a few days. Getting Chester to trust Max again would be the tough part.

On Friday afternoon he had the jumper, named Patsy Cline, in the indoor arena. He'd set up three low jumps and put them twenty feet apart. But he hadn't attempted to get her to jump them yet. He was circling the edge of the arena, warming her up.

When Abby came into the arena, Tanner rode over to her.

Abby put a hand on Patsy's bridle and rubbed her nose. "How's she doing?"

"She's a smooth ride, but I haven't taken her near the jumps yet."

"Are you sure you're the one who should be doing that? What if she throws you? It's only been three weeks since you broke your arm."

"I'll be fine. But stick around, just in case."

He urged the horse into a lope and circled the pen again, then headed for the first jump. The horse veered off as soon as she saw the jump. Tanner circled the arena, then lined Patsy up again. This time, he didn't let her have her head, and she took the jump, but she wasn't happy about it. She stopped short on the other side of it and Tanner almost flew over her head. He settled into the saddle and patted Patsy's neck.

"I know that wasn't anything personal. But I'd rather not end up in the sawdust today."

He stroked her mane and reached forward and rubbed her ears. "We're friends. You take care of me. And I'll take care of you."

He circled the arena again, then headed for the first jump. Once again, he could feel her hesitation, but she went over it and didn't stop running. He made a smaller circle around the middle of the arena, then took the jump again. Patsy cleared it with less hesitation, and he pointed her toward the second. She jumped it, but knocked the rail down. On the third jump, Patsy stopped short a few feet from the rails, and this time Tanner couldn't stay on. He went flying and landed on the other side of the jump. He landed on his back and he laid for a minute while his lungs decided whether they wanted to work or not.

Abby ran over and knelt next to him. "Dammit, Tanner."

"I'm okay." He sat up with a groan. This sawdust is a lot softer than the dirt in the pen. "At least one of us made the jump."

Abby hit him on the shoulder. "I told you not to jump her."

Tanner rubbed his shoulder. "Ow." He scowled at her. "I'm fine."

"Is your arm okay?"

"Yes. But my shoulder hurts where you punched me. " He got to his feet and brushed the sawdust from his jeans. "I thought she trusted me."

"Well, you got her over two of them."

"I guess I should've stopped there. Tomorrow, maybe you or Skyler can take her around. You guys are the experts, after all."

Abby went to get Patsy, who had wandered to the far side of the arena, while Tanner headed for the bench by the door. He sat down to finish recovering. It seemed he had fallen off more horses lately than he had in the last year.

Abby tied Patsy to a rail, then sat next to Tanner. "I came in here to tell you we can have Harper come do the six-month check up on everyone. She can check the records and give them what they need. It should keep her busy for a couple of days."

"Okay, cool. I'll let her know."

"I'm sorry she's struggling. She sure knows her herbs, though. That stuff she mixed up for Gemma worked like magic."

"Good. We need to spread the word. Let people know we trust her."

"We will. I don't want to see her fail. I like her." She glanced at him. "Have you seen her lately?"

"Not since last Sunday." He glanced at Abby, who was looking at him. "What?"

"Nothing. I think you two are cute together."

Tanner got to his feet. "We're not anything together. I just want to help her out."

"Okay. Calm down. I didn't mean anything by it."

Tanner tried to walk off the pain in his leg, which was hurt again for the third time. He stopped and looked at Abby.

"Do you think I'm a boy scout?"

She smiled. "If by that you mean sweet, respectful, and always ready to lend a hand, then yes. Why?"

Tanner shrugged. "No reason."

"Did Harper call you a boy scout?"

"Yeah."

"It's not a bad thing. And I'm sure she didn't mean it that way. She just sees what we all see in you."

He scowled. "So, you don't think it makes me a wimp?"

She laughed and got to her feet, then walked up to him and hugged him. "No. It doesn't make you a wimp. It makes you a nice guy. And this world needs more nice guys in it."

He backed away from her and wrinkled his nose. "You smell like…"

"Sour milk? Gillian spit up some milk on me this morning."

"Gross. You didn't think to change your shirt?"

"I wiped it off. I have enough laundry to do without changing my shirt every time one of the girls spills or spits something on me."

Tanner shook his head. "Man. I'm never having kids."

———— ❧ ————

Abby told Tanner they could do the six-month horse checkups by the end of the following week, so on Monday, Tanner left Harper a voicemail. When he hadn't heard back from her by Wednesday, he decided to go into town and track her down.

It was after hours, so he drove by her house first. The house was dark, and there was a 'For Rent' sign in the window. *That's not a good sign.* He continued down the road and drove the mile to the vet clinic.

There was a closed sign on the door, but Tanner could see lights on inside. He parked his truck and went to the door, then knocked. When Harper didn't come to answer it, he knocked again.

"Harper! It's Tanner. Open up."

A few moments later, he saw her through the glass door. She came from the back and she was holding a tiny black puppy in her arms. She unlocked the door and held it open.

As he stepped inside, he noticed her flushed cheeks and red eyes. "Are you okay?"

She turned and went back to the room she'd come from. He followed her and looked around the examination room. There was a couch near her desk and it had a pile of blankets on it.

He nodded toward the puppy. "Patient?"

She shook her head. "No. Somebody left him in a box outside my door this morning."

Tanner scowled. "People suck." He rubbed the puppy's ears. "Is he okay?"

"Yeah." She swiped at a tear, then kissed the puppy's head. "I feel so sorry for him."

Tanner figured the tears really didn't have much to do with the puppy, but he didn't want to call her on it. He glanced at the couch. "Are you sleeping here?"

She turned away from him as the tears started. He gave her a moment, then came up behind her and put his hands on her arms. "What can I do?"

"Get me a tissue."

He went to the desk and pulled a tissue from the holder that was in the shape of a cat. The tissues came out of its mouth, which was a little weird. He brought it to her, then took the puppy out of her hands.

"Let me take this little guy before he gets wet."

She wiped her eyes and tried discreetly to blow her nose, then tossed the tissue in the waste basket. "Just so you know. I'm not an emotional woman who cries all the time."

"Never thought you were. Sometimes, you just have to cry."

She nodded. "I'm going to keep him."

"Good. I think you could use the companionship. What are you going to call him?"

She looked at Tanner for a moment. "What's your middle name?"

"Um...Joseph."

"Okay. I'll call him Joey."

"You're going to name him after me?"

"Yes. Because you're the only person in town, well your family too, but mostly you, who doesn't think I should pack my bags and go back to the city."

"Are they still boycotting you?"

She nodded and went to pull another tissue from the cat's mouth.

"Is that why you moved out of your house?"

She wiped her eyes and nodded toward the couch. "The couch is extremely uncomfortable. But at least it isn't costing me a thousand dollars a month."

"Dammit, Harper. I told you I'd help."

"I know. I'm not out of money. But I didn't want to pay another month's rent. And since the landlord agrees with everyone else in town, he let me out of my lease. He even gave me my deposit back." She went for another tissue. "You must think I'm such a failure. A crying baby failure."

He chuckled. "I don't think that. I think you could use a stiff drink, though."

"I don't drink."

"I believe it's time you started."

Chapter Sixteen

"This just further proves my boy scout theory"

"I know it's around here somewhere."

Harper watched Tanner dig through the medicine cupboards. "Maybe he took it with him."

Tanner grinned at her over his shoulder. "Got it." He pulled a bottle of bourbon from the back of the cupboard. "It's pretty good stuff, too."

"How'd you know it was there?"

He set the bottle on the stainless steel examination table, then took two cups sitting next to the unused coffee machine. "I used to work for Dr. Benton during summer break when I was in high school."

"Because you wanted to be a vet?"

"Yeah. At the time. Until I found out how long I had to go to school for it."

He opened the bottle and poured a shot into each cup, then held one out to Harper.

She shook her head. "Really. I'm not a drinker."

"You've never had alcohol?"

"I didn't say that. I've had a margarita or two now and then."

"Tequila drinker, huh?"

"No. A margarita drinker. Occasionally."

He squinted. "You told me you only drank wine."

She shrugged. "I wasn't about to tell you I occasionally went to Margarita night."

He laughed as he continued to hold the cup out to her. "Trust me. It'll take the edge off and it won't kill you."

She rolled her eyes, then took the cup from him. She sniffed at the contents before taking a tiny sip. She frowned. "Wow. Not good."

He laughed. "Give it time." He drank from his cup, taking half the shot down in a swallow. "My dad loved bourbon. Tobias favors rum. Though he's backed way off the drinking since he's married to a physical therapist."

Harper shook her head. "What's that have to do with drinking?"

"He used the rum to self-medicate after a serious fall from a horse that messed his leg up. Gemma has changed his life in more ways than one."

She took another tiny sip of bourbon. "So falling off horses is a regular thing for you Carmichaels?"

"Not intentionally. And not that often. I've just had a bad run lately."

"Deacon must be a bourbon man like your father."

"Nope. Scotch."

"And you?"

"Beer. Not a big fan of any of the hard stuff. But it serves its purpose."

"Like when you're consoling pathetic veterinarians?"

"Yeah. But you're not pathetic. This town should be ashamed for treating you so badly. I'm inclined to hire you as our full-time vet and let everyone else deal without having one in town."

Surely he was joking. But she loved how incensed he was at the town's treatment of her. "Does the Starlight need a full-time vet?"

He smiled. "No. But it'd be worth it to teach these ranchers some manners."

Harper finished her bourbon, and Tanner poured her another shot. The last sip was certainly better than the first.

She set her cup down. "I can't."

"Sure you can. It must be working. You haven't cried in the last ten minutes."

"Stop. Don't be mean to me. I was crying about Joey." She glanced at the puppy, who was asleep in a crate. He was adorable, and Tanner was right. Joey would be a great companion to her.

"Sure you were." When a gray cat came from under the desk and sauntered over to Harper, Tanner asked, "Another stray?" He watched the cat rub against her leg.

"No. This is Shadow. He's mine."

"A city cat, huh?"

"I suppose." She picked up the cup and looked at the bourbon, then took a sip.

Tanner smiled at her. "It's growing on you, right?"

She shrugged. "Maybe a little."

He looked around the room. "How much are you paying for this place?"

"Fifteen hundred."

"Shit."

"I know. I don't know what I was thinking. Dr. Benton's been here forever, and I just thought I should take advantage of that. But of course I believed I'd actually be working on animals once in a while."

Tanner sat on the edge of the exam table and poured himself a second shot. "I have something to run by you. But you need to finish that drink and maybe one more, before you might actually listen to it."

She cocked her head. "What is it?"

"Drink."

Harper had a third shot, which was more than she'd ever drank at one time in her life. She was feeling the effects, and she sat on the table next to Tanner.

"I'm not drinking any more. So, tell me what you're going to tell me."

He slid down a foot from her and turned to face her. "Are you still determined to stay here in Connelly?"

"As depressing as this has been. Going back to Austin as a failure would be even more depressing."

"Okay. Then hear me out before you say no. And quit calling yourself a failure."

"I could just say no now and save you the trouble."

"Harper!"

She sighed. "Fine. I'm listening."

"Back when Winston first started out, he was breeding a lot of horses and he had a small barn built to use as a foaling barn. It has four nice sized stalls, and two separate rooms which aren't quite this big. The building is fully wired, has AC and heat. Fully plumbed with water to the stalls and to a sink in one of the rooms." He smiled at her. "It'd make a great and pretty funky veterinary office."

His hand was resting on the table and she put hers over it. "Are you kidding me?"

"No. I'd never. I'm serious. The barn is yours if you want it."

"So, it's at your place?"

"Yeah. Behind the barn where Lucy foaled."

"How much would the rent be?"

"No rent. The building is just sitting there empty."

"Tanner." She slid off the table and walked around it, then stopped a few feet in front of him. "Dammit. You're going to make me cry again."

He grinned. "Do you need another shot?"

"No. No more shots." She studied him for a moment. "I can't. It's too much."

"Of course you can. And if you insist on paying rent, then we'll talk about it once you start making some money."

"Does it come with a couch I can sleep on?"

He jumped off the table and put his hands on her shoulders for a moment, then circled the table himself. "I have a solution for that, too."

"Of course you do."

"You might want to sit down for this one."

Harper returned to the table and sat on it. "Okay."

"Now don't take this the wrong way. It's in no way meant to be, well, anything but... Just hear me out."

"Just tell me, Tanner." He was really cute when he was excited.

"My house. It's huge. Four bedrooms. Three upstairs. One downstairs."

"Tanner." Was he really suggesting what she thought he was suggesting?

"You could have the downstairs bedroom. It has its own bath. We'd probably never see each other."

"Oh my God. Tanner, I'd drive you crazy."

"I don't think so. Roommates. That's all. Just keep your weird food in your part of the refrigerator. And don't judge me for eating bacon and eggs for breakfast."

She picked up her cup and held it out to him. "You better pour me another shot."

Tanner laughed as he picked up the bottle and poured them each a shot. He waited until she finished hers before asking, "What do you think?"

"I think you're going to be really sorry."

"Does that mean you're going to give me a chance to be really sorry?"

She nodded. "How can I say no?"

He laughed. "Cool. Come see the barn tomorrow to make sure it's going to work out for you."

"Of course it's going to work out for me. This place. It's Dr. Benton's clinic. It's always going to be Dr. Benton's clinic. The barn will be my place."

"Damn right. And if it takes a while for everyone to come around, it doesn't matter. We can keep you pretty busy."

She slid off the table and took the cup out of his hand. She set it on the table, then returned to him and gave him a hug. "I hope you don't end up hating me."

He patted her back. "Never."

She stepped back from him. "This just further proves my boy scout theory."

"I've decided to embrace it."

"Good." She put her hands to her head. "Man. I believe I'm a bit tipsy."

"Me too." He spotted a chess board on the bookshelf. "How about another game of chess?"

"Tipsy chess?"

"Yes. Maybe I can beat you now."

"Don't count on it."

Chapter Seventeen

"But the vegan thing's a little weird, right?"

D eacon leaned forward and looked at Tanner. "You did what now?"

Tobias laughed from the couch. "Our baby brother is growing up, Deacon."

Tanner scowled at Tobias, then turned to Deacon. "Does he have to be here for this?"

Deacon nodded. "Yes." He looked at Tobias. "Behave."

Tobias shrugged. "Just stating a fact." He stretched his legs out and rested his boots on the coffee table.

Deacon looked at Tanner. "I get letting her have the barn. That's a great idea. But making her your roommate? Are you sure about that? A week ago, you could barely stand her." Tobias chuckled and Deacon shot him a look. "Just help me understand your reasoning. Because if this is something more than her being your roommate. Then her being your roommate isn't such a good idea."

Tobias put his feet on the floor and leaned forward. "Don't listen to him. This is perfect. You're going to find out real quick what's what."

Tanner looked at him. "I..." He shook his head and turned back to Deacon. "She has nowhere else to go. She gave up her house in town, because she couldn't afford to keep paying the rent with no money coming in. But she's not a freeloader. She insists on taking care of the horses there, and here, in exchange for rent. And really, this is just a courtesy conversation. I can have whoever the hell I want living in my house. The barn, sure you have a say in."

Deacon frowned and Tobias laughed again. "He has a point, Deacon. Although technically, the house belongs to the ranch."

Tanner scowled at him again.

Deacon cleared his throat. "You know the situation and the woman better than Tobias or I do. And you're old enough to make your own decisions and your own mistakes."

"So, it's okay with you? I didn't really mean that about the courtesy conversation. Of course I care what you think."

Deacon smiled. "I know, kid." He looked at Tobias. "Do you have anything to add?"

Tobias shook his head. "No. The kid appears to know what he's doing."

Tanner folded his arms across his chest. "Just how old do I need to be before you all stop referring to me as the kid?"

Deacon smiled at Tobias. "Ninety-nine? A hundred?"

Tobias laughed. "That sounds about right."

Tanner left the room and Deacon looked at Tobias. "Big mistake, right?"

"Oh, yeah."

Cassidy came into the room. "What did you two say to Tanner?"

Deacon shrugged. "Nothing. He got what he wanted. Our approval."

"He didn't look like he got what he wanted."

Tobias got to his feet. "He's just a little sensitive about being called kid."

Cassidy put her hands on her hips. "So, maybe you should stop. He's twenty-six now. And he's certainly proven himself."

Deacon stood and went to Cassidy, then put his arms around her. He kissed her on the forehead. "He knows we love him."

Tobias waved a hand at them. "I'll go make sure he's okay."

Cassidy watched him leave, then looked at Deacon. "So, what did Tanner want to talk to you about?"

Deacon sat on the edge of the desk. "He wants to offer Harper the foaling barn to use as her vet clinic."

"Oh. That's a good idea. With the way everyone has been avoiding her, I'm sure she can't afford to pay rent on the clinic and her house."

Deacon folded his arms across his chest. "Yeah. The thing is. He also offered to let her stay in the house."

Cassidy cocked her head. "Hmm. Okay. That's an interesting turn of events."

"Yeah. Strictly a roommate situation. Or so he says."

"Do you believe him?"

"I don't think he believes himself. I guess we'll see."

She moved to Deacon and put her arms around his neck. "So, Christmas wedding?"

"Shit. It wouldn't surprise me."

Tanner was in the barn feeding an apple to Precious when Tobias found him.

"I thought I might find you mucking out a stall."

"Wrong brother. That's Deacon's go to stress buster."

"Right." Tobias leaned on the gate next to Tanner. "For what it's worth, I think it's a hell of a thing you're doing for our young vet. Her setting up shop on Carmichael property just might give her the credibility she needs to win over the town."

"Damn town."

"I know. They're being narrow-minded. They see how young she is, and her purple hair. Then she offers them an alternative to pharmaceuticals and they just can't handle it. I've been spreading the word about how she helped Chance. And Gemma is thrilled with what she did for her. They'll come around. But you on her side, is going to make it happen faster. I'm proud of you."

Tanner glanced at him. "Really?"

"Yeah."

"You don't think I have ulterior motives for letting her stay at the house?"

"Nope."

Tanner sighed deeply. "I really just want to help her out."

"I know." He put a hand on Tanner's shoulder. "But it's also okay if you won't mind having her around."

Tanner turned and leaned his back against the stall. "I've never met anyone like her. She's more than purple hair and holistic medicine."

"I'm sure she is. But the vegan thing's a little weird, right?"

Tanner laughed. "Yeah. That's weird. She's living in the middle of Texas cattle country."

"Maybe you can get her to eat a steak one of these days."

"I don't know. She's pretty set in her ways."

⁂

When Harper arrived at the ranch, Tanner was waiting for her by the barn. She parked near him and got out of the truck with Joey in her arms.

"Good morning, Doc."

"Cowboy."

"Got your pal with you, I see."

"I didn't want to leave him alone at the clinic. Shadow is a little jealous and hasn't been very nice to him."

He rubbed Joey's ears, then grinned. "Let's go take a look at your new clinic."

She followed him down the drive next to the horse barn. When she saw the foaling barn, she instantly loved it. It was shaped like a classic barn, but was about half the size of a typical one. It was painted red and had a wind vane on the roof shaped like a rooster.

Tanner slid open the door, and they went inside.

Harper gasped. "Oh my gosh. This is wonderful." Joey wiggled in her arms, and she set him on the ground.

The floor had been swept clean and the three stalls had a fresh layer of straw in them. There was a big open space between the stalls and the two rooms. The first room had been set up like a kitchen with an older refrigerator and a row of cupboards over a counter. On the other side of the room was a three-foot stainless steel sink, divided in the middle. There was plenty of room to add more shelves for storage and pet crates.

Harper turned to Tanner. "I can't believe how perfect it is."

He looked around the room. "We should probably paint. And we can tile the floor if you want."

She looked at the wooden floor. "I like the wood, but tile would be easier to keep clean."

"No problem. I'll get someone to take care of that."

She took his arm. "Show me the other room."

They went to the other room and Tanner said, "Examination room, right?"

"Yes." The room was a little bigger than the first one, with space for a desk and her examination table. Dr. Benton had left all the fixtures in the office for her. She would bring everything that wasn't considered to be part of the building.

She hugged Tanner. "This is so perfect."

He stepped away from her and went to look out the window. "You'll get lots of morning sun." He turned back to her. "So. Are we doing this?"

"We're definitely doing this."

"White tile? White walls?"

"White tile, yes. But let's go with pale blue or green for the walls. I don't want it to look too sterile."

"Sounds good."

They went back to the main area, and he showed her one more door. "You even have a bathroom." He opened the door. "Probably hasn't been used in a while, so we'll have someone come check it out."

At the back of the barn was a door to a hay shed. They went into it and Harper smiled. "I can use this for my herbs."

"Yeah. Sure."

"Tanner, I love it."

"Good. I love that you love it. Now. Let me show you your room."

He picked up Joey and they walked to the house over the green grass. Rider was laying under a tree and he came to greet them. When he saw

Joey, he was very curious about who this new little visitor was. Tanner put Joey down and Rider sniffed him, then wagged his tail.

"Okay. Rider accepts him."

They left the dogs outside and went in through the kitchen door. Tanner stopped in the middle of the room. "You've seen the kitchen, of course."

"Yes. I made you coffee the morning Max brought Chester over."

"Right." He went to the living room and crossed to the far side, then opened a door. "This was Winston's room."

It was a large room with lots of windows, a big queen-sized bed, a dresser, and a woodstove with a cozy chair in the corner. Harper looked at the bed.

"He didn't die in the bed, did he?"

"No. Winston died in hospice care."

"I'm sorry. That was insensitive of me."

"It's okay. The bed's new, too. I bought it when I moved in."

"Well, of course. This is perfect too." She studied him for a moment. "Are you one hundred percent sure you want me as your roommate? Because that barn is beautiful and I'd have no problem making myself a sleeping corner out there."

"Harper. You're not sleeping in the barn."

She smiled. "Okay."

"It'll take a couple of days to get the barn ready for you to move your equipment in. But you might as well sleep here tonight. We can go get whatever you need from the clinic."

She nodded. "Thank you. I look forward to not sleeping on that hard couch tonight. But I can go get my stuff. I'm sure you have horses to whisper to."

"Yeah. A couple."

"Okay. I'll be back in a couple of hours. Do I need a key or anything?"

"The door is never locked. I don't even know where the key is."

"Okay. I forgot we were living in the country. Will you let me cook you dinner tonight to celebrate our first night as roomies?"

"Um... Is it going to be something weird I'll have to pretend I like, but actually hate?"

"No. I promise you won't hate it."

"Okay. I'll supply the beer."

She shook her head. "I'm not drinking again. I don't even remember who won the chess game last night."

"Oh, in that case, it was me."

Chapter Eighteen

"Shh. Don't jinx it."

T anner spent the afternoon working with Chester. Max would be coming in the morning to see his progress. If Chester was open to it, Tanner would get in the pen with Max and Chester and help them learn to work together again.

The sun was going down when he got Chester put away, and he headed for the kitchen door. When he walked through it, he was hit with a heavenly smell. He closed the door and stood for a moment to take it in.

Harper came in from the living room. "Welcome home, darling. Did you have a good day at work?"

Tanner pointed at her. "Funny. Are you going to take my hat and briefcase and bring me my slippers and pipe?"

"I'm very progressive. No smoking in the house."

Tanner laughed. "It smells really good in here. What are you making?"

"Tacos."

"Tacos? All the tacos I've ever eaten have had ground beef, chicken, steak, or pork in them."

"Not these." She went to the stove and stirred the pot with a wooden spoon. "It's ready whenever you are, so go do whatever you do when you come home, and let me know when you're ready to eat."

"I need ten minutes." He headed for the stairs. "I'll be right down."

He went upstairs and changed his shirt, then washed his face, his right hand, and the fingers of his left. He was really tired of wearing the cast. He also combed his hair, which he usually only did once a day in the morning.

When he returned to the kitchen, Harper had put the food on the table. There was a bowl with something resembling shredded beef. Another had yellow and green salsa. He recognized the cucumbers and the avocado slices, but he wasn't sure what the yellow chunks were. Some sort of fruit. There was a third bowl with black beans, another with seasoned rice, and a plate with flour tortillas.

He sat and took a sip of the beer she'd put by his plate. "Wow. This is quite the spread. House rules are the cook has to wash their own dishes."

"I figured. Build yourself a taco and let me know what you think."

"Okay." He picked up a tortilla and spooned some of the 'meat' mixture into it. "So what is this?"

"Jackfruit."

"Excuse me?"

"Jackfruit. It has a similar texture to shredded beef. Or so I've been told. But watch out, I make it pretty spicy."

"I like spicy." He added a layer of black beans and then topped it off with the salsa. He took a bite while Harper watched him. "Mmm." He chewed and swallowed. "Wow."

"Good wow? Or bad wow?"

"Really good wow."

She clapped her hands. "Yay! Try the rice."

"Yes, ma'am." He pointed at the cubes of yellow fruit in the salsa. "What's this?"

"Mango."

"Oh, okay. I like mango."

Everything was delicious, and he ate four tacos and two servings of rice before he had to stop. He washed down his last bite with the end of his beer. "I'm super impressed. I had no idea I could enjoy a meal this much without meat in it."

"I'm so glad you liked it. This doesn't mean I'm going to eat a fresh Carmichael steak, though."

He laughed. "I know. I'd never ask you to compromise your chosen way of life."

She stood and started clearing the table. Tanner watched her for a moment, then got up to help her. "New house rule. He who enjoys the meal has to help with the dishes."

"Thank you. I hate doing dishes."

"Me too. I usually eat right from the pot whenever possible."

"That's kind of disgusting."

"Not when it's just me eating from it."

"No. It's still disgusting."

She ran a sink full of soapy water and Tanner stood by with a towel. "I'm not so good with the washing part. But I'm pretty good at drying."

She glanced at him. "Didn't you have to do the dishes when you were a kid?"

"No."

"I thought all kids had chores like dishes."

"Not when you have a full time cook. My chores were mucking stalls and feeding the animals. My favorite thing was collecting the eggs, but Abby usually got to them before me."

"Do you have chickens here?"

"No. But at the main house they have about thirty chickens. They produce enough eggs to keep everyone supplied." He nudged her. "And like milking cows, it's not exploiting them. They lay eggs whether anyone's eating them or not. If we didn't eat them, the raccoons, snakes, and foxes would. And if we let them all grow into chicks, we'd be overrun with chickens, which would also get eaten by the foxes."

She handed him a rinsed plate. "So, even rich kids have chores?"

"We did. And the new crop of Carmichaels do."

"Good. I like that. That's why you don't act like a rich kid."

"It's nice to have the money. But we try not to let it define us. Except every September fifteenth."

"What happens on September fifteenth?"

"The Starlight Gala. It's hosted by Deacon and Cassidy. Before them, my mother did it. Before her, my grandmother. In Abby's words, it's an elitist show of money and power. There is a very exclusive guest list. Everyone from the Texas Ten, of course. And a few select guests who are deemed worthy."

"Wow. That doesn't sound like the Carmichaels I've met."

"Deacon and Cassidy have toned it down a bit over the last seven years. But Mother was quite traditional. She liked the decorum and the properness of it all."

"Was she from one of the rich families?"

"No. Her family was not wealthy. They did fine. Her brothers still run the family ranch. Ten thousand acres or so. But she wasn't who my grandparents expected their only son to marry."

"Yikes. How'd that turn out?"

"Fortunately, my grandparents weren't assholes, and they welcomed her into the family."

"And neither of your brothers married women from rich ranching families?"

"No. Well, Cassidy's grandfather was fairly well off. But she grew up in Austin. I don't think Gemma had ever been on a ranch until she came here to be Cassidy's maid of honor."

"That's how she and Tobias met?"

"Sort of. That's a story for another day. Let's get these dishes done and then take a walk. There's a full moon tonight."

───────※───────

They did the dishes, then Harper picked up Joey. Tanner took a flashlight, and they went through the kitchen door, with Rider following close behind. They crossed the yard, went past the barn, and headed to the meadow beyond the pens. Tanner opened the gate, then closed it behind them.

Harper put Joey down, and he ran after Rider. It seemed in one day, they'd become friends. Tanner took Harper's arm and shone the light in front on the grass in front of them.

"Got to watch out for horse apples." He stopped walking and looked at the ground around them, then turned off the light. "Okay, look up at the sky."

Harper looked up and gasped. "Oh my gosh. I've never seen this many stars before."

"We have an extra layer of them here in northern Texas."

She laughed. "It seems you do."

"Do you want to sit?"

"Sure." They sat in the grass and the dogs came over and laid down in front of them. "You have a beautiful place here, Tanner."

"It's special alright." He dropped back onto the grass, put a hand behind his head, and bent his knees. Harper laid next to him and he nudged her thigh. "First one to see a falling star gets the last piece of apple pie in the fridge."

"Challenge accepted. I love apple pie." They lay for several minutes watching the stars, then Harper glanced at Tanner. "I believe we're getting along now, cowboy."

"Shh. Don't jinx it." She laughed, then he nudged her again and pointed at the sky. "Falling star!"

"Oh, man."

"If you keep being nice to me, I'll share the pie with you."

They stayed another fifteen minutes, then Tanner sat up. "The grass is getting dewy."

Harper sat too. "I guess I'm about ready for some apple pie."

He stood, then held a hand out to her and pulled her to her feet. He pulled a little too hard, and she bumped right into him. She took a step back.

"Whoops. Sorry."

"No worries. My fault." He turned the flashlight on and they headed back for the house. Joey was having trouble keeping up, so Harper picked him up and carried him the rest of the way. They went into the kitchen and Harper took Joey to her room to put him in his crate for the night. When she returned, Tanner had warmed the single piece of pie and set it in the middle of the table.

Harper sat down, and he took a carton of vanilla ice cream from the freezer. "Normally, I'd eat right out of the carton. But since you think that's disgusting, I'll put some in a bowl."

"Thank you."

He scooped some ice cream into the bowl, then returned the carton to the freezer. He sat down and looked at the pie. "You have to at least be tempted to eat apple pie à la mode."

"Actually, if ever I was tempted. That's the one thing that'd do it."

He cut off a bite of pie and then some ice cream. "It's the best thing in the world."

"I'm sure it is." She took a bite of pie. "Is there anything your Ruthie can't make?"

"I don't think so." He took another bite. "Tomorrow I'll go by Johnson's and get some paint, unless you want to pick it out yourself."

"Just pale blue or green. Either is fine."

"Okay. And I'll have one of the men get it painted for you."

"I'm sure your men have better things to do. I'll paint. I actually love to paint."

"Okay. Do you love to tile floors, too?"

"No. That you can have someone do."

"Once that's done, we can move the stuff over from town."

"I'm very excited to get set up. Even if no one comes to see me."

"They will. Sooner or later. But until then. We've got a barn full of horses needing various things."

"I'm on it. I'll look at your records in the morning and bring what I need from the clinic."

He pushed the plate with the last little bit of pie on it toward her. "And when you're done here, you can go check on the horses at the main house."

"Perfect."

"We also have sheep, goats, pigs, and llamas."

"I'll check out everyone."

"Just watch out for the llamas, they're kind of mean."

"Why do you have llamas? You don't eat them, do you?"

Tanner laughed. "No. Of course not. They make great watchdogs. They keep the predators away from the sheep, goats, and pigs."

"Interesting."

"Plus, they're pretty cool animals. As long as you don't get too close to them."

Chapter Nineteen

"Time to get back on the horse, Harper."

The next two weeks were busy, and Tanner didn't see a lot of Harper. She spent her mornings with the horses, and her afternoons getting her clinic ready. She also had a few customer call her and she'd made a few house calls and two clinic visits to her partially finished clinic. When he did see her, she seemed happy and their living situation was working out fine.

On Saturday morning, she came into the kitchen while he was drinking a cup of coffee.

She smiled at him. "Good morning, roomie."

"Doctor."

She noticed his cast was gone and he was wearing a removable brace. "Hey. You got it off."

"Yeah. Finally." He looked at the brace. "He said to wear this for two more weeks, but that's probably not going to happen."

"You should listen to your doctor." She took a pitcher with a green concoction she'd mixed up and poured some into a glass.

Tanner frowned at it. "I'm sorry. I know that's probably really healthy. But it's just not right drinking something green."

"Do you want to try it before you judge it?"

"No. I can smell it. I don't want to try it."

She put the pitcher away and took a sip of her drink. "Mmm. Delicious."

"What's in it?"

"Kale, carrots, celery, and apple, and some whey."

"Gross, gross, gross, not gross, and I have not idea what whey is."

"You know it wouldn't hurt you to eat a vegetable once in a while."

"If managed this long to get by with minimal vegetable consumption." He watched her take a drink. "What are your plans today?"

"Absolutely nothing. I was so excited to get the clinic set up, I finished early. I'll be officially open on Monday. I even have two appointments."

"Wow. Congratulations."

"It helped quite a bit when word got out that the Carmichaels trusted me with their Andalusians. Not to mention my clinic is on their ranch." She pointed at him. "You saved me, Tanner."

"It was my pleasure. I'm glad it's working out."

"And here we are, almost two weeks in and I haven't driven you crazy."

"I believe I'm getting used to you."

Joey came into the kitchen, ran to the door, and barked. Harper let him and Rider outside.

"Why did you ask what my plans were?"

"I thought we might take a ride."

"In the truck?"

He laughed. "No. On horses."

She shook her head. "I love horses. I love taking care of them. And petting them. But riding them, not so much."

"Harper. You can't live on a ranch and not ride a horse. Have you ever ridden a horse?"

"Yes. It wasn't a great experience, and I never got on another one."

"Haven't you heard the saying, when you fall off a horse, you need to get right back on?"

"That's a bicycle."

"Same principal. What happened with you and the horse?"

"I fell off."

"That's it?"

She scowled at him. "Isn't that enough?"

"I've fallen off three horses since you've known me."

"Three? I only know about two."

"That's beside the point. I keep getting back on. How old were you?"

"Twelve."

He cocked his head. "Time to get back on the horse, Harper."

She sighed. "I suppose it is."

"Right after lunch."

"You'll help me, right? And not make fun of me?"

"Of course. And I'd never."

She smiled. "I know. Fine. Right after lunch."

He finished his coffee and set the cup in the sink. "I'll see you then."

"You need to wash your cup out."

"Don't be a nag."

"We could go before lunch. Do you want me to pack us a picnic? We can eat on the trail like real cowpokes?"

"Sure, as long as it isn't green. And you stop calling me a cowpoke."

Harper met Tanner at the barn with a picnic lunch in a canvas tote. When he tried to look in the bag, she pulled it away from him. "No, it's a surprise."

"I'm going hungry today, aren't I?"

"No. Have some faith."

Tanner walked to Mariah, a very laid back horse some of the kids had ridden. He put a hand on the saddle. "This is a horse."

"Okay. Is that what you call it?"

He waved her over. "Come here. Do you remember how to get on?'

"Of course." She moved to the horse and studied it for a moment, then put her foot in the stirrup and threw her other leg over the saddle. "Are you impressed?"

"A little bit, yeah." He mounted Peso.

"Isn't that the horse that tossed you the day we met?"

"Yes. Right after you honked your horn."

"Right. I guess I was partially responsible."

"Partially?"

"Are we going to talk? Or are we going to ride?"

Tanner clicked his tongue, and both horses started walking. It caught Harper off-guard, and she gasped, and grabbed the saddle horn.

Tanner glanced at her. "You know that's not a handle, right?"

She let go of it and put both hands on the reins. "I know." She and Mariah followed Tanner and Peso out of the barn. They headed across the gravel area in front of the barns, then through a gate to the pasture.

Tanner glanced at Harper. "Still on, I see."

"Don't make me sorry I agreed to this."

They continued across the pasture and came to another fence. Tanner opened the gate, and they went through it. They'd now have miles of open grassland to ride across.

Tanner glanced at Harper. She was doing fine and seemed relaxed. "How're you feeling?"

"Good. This horse is very sweet."

"Yes, she is."

"So, how far could we ride and still be on Carmichael land?"

"All the way to Oklahoma."

She laughed, then realized he wasn't joking. "Oh, wow. And why would someone need that much land? You can't possible use it all."

"We move the herd around every season. It keeps the grass healthy. We also don't overgraze. We run around 10,000 head on natural grasslands.

"That's a lot of cows."

"I really don't know too much about that part of things. That's Tobias' area. He takes care of the cattle. Which is great. Because I hate cows."

"You hate them?"

"Well, I hate dealing with them. They're dumb and can get themselves in trouble faster than a fox in a henhouse."

"So, you don't whisper to cows?"

"Not if I can help it."

They rode on without much conversation, and after an hour, Tanner headed for a grove of cottonwoods. "There's a creek running through those trees. We can eat lunch there."

They got to the creek and Tanner dismounted, then held Mariah's halter while Harper got down. She walked to the edge of the creek, which was about ten feet wide and only a foot or so deep.

"This is beautiful."

Tanner handed her the lunch tote. "Your mystery lunch."

They sat down in the grass near the creek, and Harper handed him a sandwich in a plastic bag. He looked at it.

"It's green."

She laughed. "I couldn't resist. It's avocado—which Abby said you liked—lettuce, and I even added bacon to yours."

He took the sandwich out of the bag and looked at it. "Hmm. Okay. It looks good. What's on yours?"

"Avocado, lettuce, and tomato. Abby also said you weren't a fan of tomatoes."

"That's right, I'm not. But they're from Gemma's greenhouse, so they're probably as good as a tomato can be."

She took a bite. "Wonderful. What all do you raise to eat on the Starlight Ranch?"

"Cows, pigs, the occasional lamb, but Abby and I won't eat lamb. Chickens. We have meat chickens and laying hens. And Gemma, Ruthie, and Abby all have gardens."

"Cassidy doesn't have a garden?"

"Ruthie has that covered. Cassidy helps her out, though. When Ruthie lets her."

"So, you're pretty self-sufficient."

"Yeah."

"No milk cows?"

"No. My mother had a few when Deacon was a kid. But there was too much other stuff to deal with, so when the cows aged out, she never replaced them. The last one died about fifteen years ago."

They finished their sandwiches and washed them down with bottled water, then Tanner took the horses to the creek to drink.

"Do you want to go a bit further? Or are you ready to head back?"

"I'd like to stay out a while longer."

"Good."

"I need to use the lady's room though, first."

Tanner nodded toward the trees. "Just pick a tree."

"Thanks."

She wandered off into the trees and Tanner checked the horse's tack to make sure they were ready to ride. When he heard Harper say something, he stopped to listen.

"Are you okay?"

"I need you to come here."

"Um... I hope you don't need help with whatever you were doing over there."

"Just come here."

She sounded alarmed, so Tanner headed for her. When he came around the bushes she was behind, he stopped short.

"Shit." A very large mountain lion was thirty feet away. He looked at Tanner and snarled. "Okay." He reached for Harper's arm and pulled her in behind him, then he made eye contact with the big cat. The cat didn't seem to like that, and he snarled again and took a step toward them. "So, my mojo doesn't work on mountain lions." Tanner glanced around. They didn't have too many options. And climbing a tree to get away from a cat seemed pointless.

Harper whispered in his ear. "What are we going to do?"

"I'm working on that."

She put a hand on his back. "Work faster. He looks really mad."

"If he charges me. Run like hell for the horses and take Peso to go get help."

"That's a terrible plan."

He glanced back at her. "I'm open for suggestions."

"How about we both run like hell?"

Tanner looked at the cat again. "He'll just chase us. You know how cats are. If they see something running, that's when the fun starts."

"Can the horses outrun him?"

"No."

"So we just stand here?"

Tanner shrugged. "As long as we don't make a move, he shouldn't attack."

"Shouldn't?"

Tanner scowled at the cat. "I'm just winging it here. I've never faced down a cougar before." He tried connecting with the cat again. "Why don't you mosey on? We won't hurt you as long as you don't hurt us."

The cat snarled again, and Harper took Tanner's arm and whispered. "I don't think he likes you talking to him." Tanner slowly took his cell phone out of his pocket. "Are you going to text him?"

"Shhh. I have an ideal." He opened the clock app and set off the alarm. The cat jumped, then turned and ran away. "That's the same way I feel about alarm clocks."

He watched the cat disappear into the brush, then turned to Harper. She threw her arms around his neck. She was trembling, and he held her close.

"Okay. It's fine. We're fine."

"You rescued me again."

"We should go in case he decides to come back." She kept her arms around his neck, but leaned back a few inches and looked at him.

"Sorry. I was really scared."

"You didn't seem that scared."

"I talk when I'm nervous."

"I see." She still had her arms around his neck, and it didn't seem like she was going to let go anytime soon. But he was fine with that. He put his hands on her hips and pulled her in a little tighter. She didn't resist, and he smiled at her. "What's happening here?"

She was slightly breathless. "I don't know."

"I'd really like to kiss you right now."

"Well, maybe you should stop talking about it and do it."

He pulled her in even closer, then leaned in and kissed her. He hadn't kissed a lot of women, but he wasn't a novice either. He knew what a good kiss felt like. And that was a hell of a kiss. He moved his hands to her back and tightened his grip before kissing her again.

He nuzzled her neck. "Harper?"

She whispered in his ear, "Yeah?"

"Is this just because you were scared of the mountain lion?"

She kissed his neck, then moved to his cheek before returning to his mouth. Then she looked at him. "No. I've been wanting to do this for quite some time."

He grinned. "Really?"

"Quit gloating and kiss me again."

He kissed her, then forced himself to take a step back. "Seriously, the cat could return. We need to go."

She nodded. "Can we continue this when we're safely back home?"

"You betcha." He took her hand, and they headed for the horses. When they got back, the horses were nervous. Tanner tried to calm them down. "He's gone. You're fine." They calmed at the sound of his voice. But it also meant the cat had probably kept running. If it was still around, the horses would let him know.

He turned to Harper and took her in his arms again. "Do you still want to ride farther?"

She shook her head. "No. I think I want to go home now. We have some business to attend to."

"That we do." He backed her up against Peso and kissed her again. Peso whinnied and bobbed his head. Tanner laughed. "Get your own girl, Peso."

Chapter Twenty

"This is my favorite shirt."

T he ride back to the ranch seemed a lot longer than the ride to the creek had been. Harper was anxious to get home. She'd made her move, and it seemed Tanner was one hundred percent on board. She hadn't planned on making a move. She wasn't even aware she wanted to. But when she found herself in his arms, it all became clear. She was in love with the boy scout cowboy.

She glanced at him and tried to read what was on his mind. He'd been quiet. But when he looked at her, he smiled. "Almost there."

"I thought maybe we got lost."

He grinned. "Once we get past those aspens, you'll see the house and the outbuildings. I haven't gotten lost since I was eleven."

"What happened?"

"I figured I was old enough to take my horse out by myself. Deacon told me not to, but I went anyway." He laughed. "It took him and Tobias two hours to find me."

"Were you in trouble?"

"Deacon figured the experience put the fear of God in me, and that was enough punishment."

"I like Deacon. He did a good job with you and Abby."

"I suppose he did."

They reached the aspens and wound their way through them. Then, like Tanner had said, Harper could see ranch buildings ahead at the bottom of the grassy hill they were on.

Tanner stopped Peso and Mariah stopped, as well. "I don't suppose you want to try a little run down the hill to the barn?"

"Is Mariah capable of running?"

"She'll do her best to keep up with Peso."

"Okay. But not too fast."

"I'll keep it in third." Tanner clicked his tongue and urged Peso into a trot and then a lope. He glanced back at Harper, who was close behind him. She held on and managed to catch him. They pulled up as they got close to the barn, then walked the rest of the way to Skyler, who was out front.

He took Mariah's halter as Harper got down. "I didn't think Mariah had it in her." He rubbed her nose. "Good girl."

Harper kissed the side of Mariah's head. "Thank you for not letting me fall off."

Skyler looked at Tanner. "How was the ride?"

"Ran into a mountain lion."

"What? Shit. What happened?"

"Harper walked up on it. When I got to her, the cat was about fifty feet away."

"How'd you get rid of it?"

He glanced at Harper. "Used the alarm on my phone. I figured and hoped the sound would scare it off. And It did."

"Good call. So I assumed you tried talking to it first?"

Tanner grinned. "Of course. I had to try. Now I know. My skills don't work on predators."

Skyler patted his shoulder. "I'm glad you're safe. You need to give Tobais a heads up. They're moving the herd soon."

"I'll call him now." He looked at Harper. "We'll put the horses away. Go relax. This has been an interesting day."

She smiled. "Yes, it has. I think I'll go take a shower."

Tanner watched her walk away, then realized Skyler was probably wondering why he was so interested. He turned to Skyler and took out his phone. "I'll call Tobias."

"I'll put your horses away for you." He looked at Tanner for a moment. "Did something else happen out there today?"

Tanner shook his head. "No. Isn't being threatened by a mountain lion enough?"

"Sure. That's plenty."

He led the two horses into the barn, and Tanner sighed. Skyler knew him too well after working together for seven years. He took out his phone and dialed Tobias.

"Little brother. What's up?"

"I was just riding about five miles north of the house and came face to face with a cougar."

"*Gato monte*, huh? Shit. That's too close. What happened? Are you okay?"

"Yeah. I scared it off. But he's bound to cause trouble."

"I'll have some of the men track him down. Where were you, exactly?"

"We were at the creek by the stand of cottonwoods. Winston's favorite fishing spot in the spring when the water's high."

"I know the place."

"I don't suppose the men can trap him and move him. He was a beautiful cat."

Tobias laughed. "I'll instruct the men to attempt to capture and move. But no guarantees. Their safety is my number one priority."

"I understand. Just...if it's possible."

"Got it Dr. Doolittle."

"Okay. I've got to go."

"See you tomorrow morning for breakfast."

Tanner helped Skyler with the horses, then headed for the house. He wasn't quite sure what he was going to find there. The kissing had been spontaneous, but somehow it felt like it was a long time coming. He found Harper sitting at the kitchen table with Abby. She was wearing one of his western cut shirts and a pair of denim shorts.

He pointed at her. "That's my shirt."

She smiled at him. "Sorry. I was supposed to be doing laundry today. But instead we went on a trail ride and hung out with a pretty kitty."

Abby got up and hugged him. "Scary afternoon."

He glanced at Harper over Abby's shoulder, and she raised her eyebrows and grinned. "Yeah. I told Tobias about the cat and asked if the men could trap him instead of shooting him. It's really not his fault he wandered onto our land."

Abby patted his cheek. "That's sweet." She returned to the table. "Do you want some tea?"

Tanner answered her by retrieving his coffee cup from the sink and filling it with coffee. "That's like asking me if I want a cup of Kool-Aid. Actually, I'd drink Kool-Aid before I'd drink tea."

Harper picked up her tea and took a sip. "What do you have against tea?"

"It's basically hot water that tastes bad."

Abby laughed. "I think Tanner started drinking coffee when he was fifteen. He's a hardcore coffee man." She glanced at him. "It's probably what stunted his growth."

Tanner stepped forward and messed up Abby's hair. "I'm taller than you."

She pulled away from him. "You smell like horses. Go take a shower."

"I always smell like horses. As do you. Except when you smell like used milk."

She scowled at him. "I most certainly do not."

Tanner leaned against the counter to finish his coffee. "Don't you have kids to get home to?"

"We're going soon. I'm consoling my friend."

He looked at Harper. "Do you need consoling?"

"I need to drink a cup of tea with my friend."

Tanner returned his cup to the sink. "I'm going to go take a shower."

When he finished his shower, he returned to the kitchen in a pair of jeans and a white t-shirt. Harper was there, still at the table, with an empty tea cup.

He sat across from her. "Did my sister finally leave?"

"Yes. Are you hungry? I can make you something. Or warm up one of Ruthie's meals."

He shook his head. "Not hungry."

She got up and went to the refrigerator, then opened the door. Tanner stood and came up behind her. He put his hands on her hips and she turned around to face him.

"Hey cowboy."

"Doctor. It seems we started something today."

"Yes we did."

He pulled her in closer and she put her hands on his shoulders. "You're wearing my shirt."

"It was hanging in the laundry room. I didn't go get it from your closet."

"Yeah. That'd be a little rude." He moved his hands to the front of the shirt and unsnapped the top button. "This is my favorite shirt."

"Hmm. You probably want it back, then."

"I wouldn't mind." He popped another snap. "We could go up to my room and find you a different one. One that isn't my favorite."

She nodded. "We could." She pulled the rest of the snaps open. "Or I could give it back to you right here and now."

He put his hands inside the shirt on her waist. Her skin was warm, and he felt her tremble under his touch. He leaned in and kissed her, and she put her hands around his neck. "I'd still like to go up to my room."

She kissed him before stepping back and taking his hand. "My room's closer."

They ran across the living room to her door and when she opened it, Shadow ran out. Harper squealed, then laughed as the cat ran under the couch. Tanner pushed her through the door and closed it, backing up until they reached the bed.

Tanner looked at her for a moment. "Are you sure about this?"

She took off the shirt and dropped it on the floor.

Tanner nodded. "Okay."

─────────── ❖ ───────────

Tanner kissed Harper, then brushed some hair off her forehead, before pulling the blanket over them and laying down next to her.

"So that just happened."

She giggled. "My goodness. It certainly did." She turned toward him and threw her leg over his. "I should've borrowed your shirt a long time ago."

"My brothers and Abby, they all talk about the fireworks in a relationship. They say the fireworks are everything." He kissed Harper's neck. "Now I know what they're talking about."

"I felt it too. Like the Fourth of July."

"Exactly."

She tilted her head up to look at him. "What does it mean?"

He kissed her. "I'm pretty sure it means you're my fireworks person. And that means you're stuck with me."

"I think I'm alright with that. There's just one thing. And this is totally selfish of me. But can we keep this between the two of us for a little while?"

"I'd rather go shout it from the rooftop. But sure. May I ask why?"

"Well, the people of Connelly are starting to come around. Slowly, but they're coming."

"And sleeping with a Carmichael will undermine your professional status."

She laid her head on his chest. "Never mind. That's totally unfair to you."

"No. I get it. You need to be taken seriously. Maybe we could slowly start being seen together."

"Like dating?"

"Yeah. Like dating."

"I like that. As long as when we're here at home, we let the fireworks fly."

Tanner laughed. "I'm pretty sure I can get behind this plan." He rolled onto his side and pulled her in close. "Speaking of which..."

Harper laughed. "Let's go for the grand finale."

Chapter Twenty-One

"We bonded over the elitist snobbery of it all."

Abby crawled into bed next to Skyler and snuggled up to him. "How is it so cold in the middle of August? She pulled Skyler's grandmother's quilt up to her neck.

"The Farmer's Almanac is predicting an early winter with exceptionally cold weather."

"Snow?"

"Most likely."

They both stopped talking for a moment when they heard one of the girls through the baby monitor. She fussed a little, then quieted down. Abby and Skyler relaxed.

She kissed Skyler's neck and settled into his side. "Has Tanner seemed weird to you lately?"

"Weird how?"

"I think something is going on between him and Harper. He hasn't complained about her in weeks."

Skyler took a few moments to consider it. "He was acting a little strange today when they came back from their ride. But it probably had something to do with the mountain lion. That'd make anyone act weird."

"Hmm. No. That's not it. I think they're doing it."

Skyler laughed. "No way."

"Why not?"

"I don't know. They're both so...innocent."

Abby shook her head. "It's always the quiet ones you need to watch out for."

He raised onto an elbow. "Speaking of doing it...it appears the girls are down for the night."

"It does seem that way."

"When are you going to let me talk you into having another kid?"

She put a hand on his chest. "Whoa there, cowboy. The whole twin thing was a surprise. A wonderful one. But what if it happened again?"

"It's very unlikely to happen again."

"Still. And they just started consistently sleeping through the night."

"And a year from now, they'll be old pros."

"And we will have been sleeping gloriously through the night. Or not sleeping a lot more often, if and when we desire, all that time. A newborn will start the cycle all over again."

He sighed. "Alright, I get it."

She patted his chest. "I know you want a big family. And God knows, we've got to keep up with the Carmichaels. Ask me again in six months. Just give me six months of sleeping through the night."

"Fine. But in the meantime..."

"We need to take advantage of our sleeping daughters."

"Yes."

He leaned down and kissed her. "We at least have to beat Tobias."

"Yeah, yeah, yeah."

When Tanner got to the main house, everyone else was already there. All fifteen of them, including baby Luna, turned to look at him when he came into the dining room. As more and more kids were added to the family, they moved to the formal dining room and put a second table in for the kids to sit at.

Tanner took his seat next to Abby. "Sorry. I overslept."

Abby nudge Skyler, then turned to Tanner. "We all managed to get here on time hauling kids with us."

"I said I was sorry."

Deacon held up his mimosa. "Now that everyone is here. I have an announcement."

Tanner shook his head. "Who's pregnant now?"

Deacon laughed. "No one that I know of. Except for Gemma, of course. This is about the gala. Everything is officially done for this year's gala weekend. The planning, reserving, ordering, and inviting is all done." He frowned when no one responded, so Cassidy and Gemma started clapping, and Tobias whistled. "That's better." He took a drink. "And it's all due to my beautiful and talented wife, who was also juggling four kids." He kissed Cassidy. "I'm damn proud of you."

"I had a lot of help from Gemma."

"When I wasn't throwing up." Gemma smiled at Tanner. "But thanks to Harper, that seems to be behind me now."

Abby turned to Tanner. "You should bring her to the gala."

"Um…I guess I could do that." He wanted to change the subject. If he started thinking about Harper and talking about her, he wouldn't be able to hide the giddiness he was still feeling. And everyone would know just what happened last night. "Who's chasing the hounds this year?"

All the adults except for Gemma raised their hands, who looked at Tanner. "Is Harper a good enough rider to enter?"

He shook his head. "No. Yesterday was the first time since she was twelve that she'd been on a horse."

"Maybe by next year. If she keeps hanging around you, she's bound to become a good rider."

Tobias raised a hand. "Okay. I want to hear about everyone's favorite gala and why."

Deacon smiled at Cassidy. "Nine years ago."

Tobias nodded. "Yeah, yeah. We all know why." He took Gemma's hand. "Mine was eight years ago when I got to take Gemma. The why is…because I got to take Gemma. I finally had a date."

Gemma bumped her shoulder into his. "I guess I have to go with that one, too. I should've tried the spiked punch that year, because I've been pregnant or nursing every year since." She frowned. "I've never had the spiked punch."

Cassidy laughed. "You're not missing anything." She looked at Abby and Skyler. "How about you guys?"

Skyler put his arm around Abby. "I think we'd both go with nine years ago, as well. Your mother re-introduced us. And excluding a couple months of me being an idiot. We've been together ever since."

Abby kissed his cheek. "We bonded over the elitist snobbery of it all."

Deacon laughed. "Seems that was a momentous gala for all of us." He glanced toward the kids' table. "And look where it led us."

Abby patted Tanner's hand. "It wasn't momentous for Tanner."

He smiled. "Sure it was. It was my first gala. I'll always remember it."

Abby nudged him. "Maybe this year will be even more momentous for you."

"I guess we'll see."

Tanner knew Abby was trying to get him to make some sort of confession about Harper. But they'd agreed to keep things to themselves, so that's what he'd do. It was actually kind of nice having a secret from the rest of the family. Usually, everybody knew everybody's business. Now if they'd just stop bringing her up, everything would be fine.

Deacon looked at Tanner. "You could start bringing Harper to Sunday breakfast. She is living in your house, which kind of makes her family."

They just won't stop. Tanner shrugged. "I guess. She doesn't really eat any of this stuff. But I'll tell her she's welcome."

Cassidy drank some of her orange juice. "I'm sure Ruthie could accommodate her diet."

"Yeah. Like I said, I'll let her know." He picked up his fork. "So, any word on the cougar?"

Since there were so many of them, every Sunday, one family would help Ruthie with the cleanup. When everyone left the dining room, Skyler picked up some plates, then smiled at Abby. "You're right. They're doing it."

Abby laughed. "So obvious."

Tanner came back into the room. "Do you guys need help?"

Abby cocked her head. "Only if it doesn't mean you expect us to help you next week when it's your turn."

"My offer comes with no ties."

"In that case, adios some plates."

Tanner picked up a load of plates and headed for the kitchen behind Abby. They both unloaded next to the sink, then Abby took Tanner's arm.

"I'm serious about you bringing Harper to the gala. I think she'd have fun and meet some rancher who could be her future customers."

"Yeah. I'm going to ask her. She'll probably side with you on the snobbery of it all."

"I guarantee she will. And tell her I'd love to help her find a dress. I am the gala dress expert, after all."

"Yes, you are. You still think it's an elitist show of power and money, right?"

"Yes. But I know my role. Besides, it's so fun going as the Carmichael who married a Fremont. Seven years later, they still talk about it."

"The town is still a little divided on that."

"That's why it's so fun."

"One of these years, his parents are going to show up again."

"Nah. I don't think so. They've boycotted it ever since Skyler and I got married. But interestingly enough, his mother reached out to him a couple of weeks ago. She really wants to meet the girls."

"It's about damn time. They're two-years-old."

"He's thinking about it. But he really doesn't want to subject the girls to his parent's behavior. He hasn't forgiven them. And I don't blame him."

"Me either. I say screw them. But I'm not a dad and I don't have crazy parents who disowned me. So I guess I don't really have a say."

"That's why I stay out of it. But if it was my decision, I'd say screw them, too."

Skyler walked into the kitchen. "Are you talking about my parents?"

Abby went to him and took the dirty dishes from him. "I'm sorry."

He shrugged. "Don't be. You have every right to feel however you want to feel about them. And I've decided not to introduce my mother to Gillian and Gianna. Not until my dad makes some sort of effort to settle things. He'll never admit he was wrong. But give me something. Anything to show he at least has a little regret for what he did."

Abby hugged him. "You can always revisit the idea in a year or two."

Skyler nodded. "It'll always be out there. We're bound to run into them some day with the kids in tow."

"We'll deal with that when and if it happens."

Tanner leaned on the counter. "When Deacon got ready to make his announcement, I thought for sure it was about you two having another kid."

Abby patted Skyler's chest. "We're currently in negotiations."

"Well, good luck with that. I'm counting on you two to win the baby battle. We can't let Tobias come out on top."

Skyler laughed. "He's still playing catch up to Deacon."

Ruthie came into the kitchen and frown at them. "Leaning on the counter and standing around talking about adding more babies to the Carmichael clan isn't getting the dishes done."

Tanner pushed away from the counter. "This is where I take my leave."

Abby scowled at him. "You said you were going to help."

"I helped clear the table." He left the room, and Ruthie turned to Abby and Skyler.

"How long before that boy and his young doctor friend start adding their own babies to the mix?"

Abby laughed. "Ruthie, what do you know that we don't know?"

"There's nothing to know. It's clear as day. Young Tanner is finally in love."

Chapter Twenty-Two

"I'm not going to share my one thing."

They'd taken in a horse that was having trouble adjusting to its new home, and Tanner and Skyler spent a few hours trying to get him to settle down. At eight, Tanner insisted Skyler go home to Abby and the girls. Then he spent another half-hour in the barn. The horse finally seemed to calm down, and Tanner felt comfortable leaving him. Though he knew he'd have to come check on him before he went to bed. Otherwise, he wouldn't be able to sleep.

Tanner came into the kitchen with Rider, who'd been in the barn with him. The dog checked his bowl for food, drank some water, then went to lie down on his bed in the corner. Joey came in from the living room and greeted Tanner, then laid next to Rider. They'd become inseparable. And whenever Rider went outside without him, Joey seemed to think he was never going to see his friend again. Rider gave him a couple of licks before rolling onto his side with a contented sigh. Joey curled up next to him.

Tanner filled a glass with water and leaned against the counter while he drank it. He'd come in for a quick dinner while Skyler was still there. So he wasn't hungry. But a snack might be nice.

Harper sauntered into the room with a smile. "Are you in for the night?"

"Yep. Well, maybe." When she cocked her head at him, he added, "Probably."

She crossed the room to him and took off his hat, then kissed him. "Good." She hung his hat on a hook by the door. "Does that popcorn thingy hanging on the fireplace work? Or is it for decoration only?"

"Well, I didn't go buy it to look homey, if that's what you mean. It came with the place."

"Have you ever used it?"

"No."

She smiled slyly. "Can we try it out?"

"You eat popcorn?"

"Of course I eat popcorn. You've seen me eat corn on the cob."

"Right. Popcorn is corn. A vegetable that doesn't have a face. Even though it has ears."

She shook her head. "You can only use that once. And, actually, it wasn't that funny the first time."

He pushed away from the counter and walked over to her, then he put his arms around her. "Come on. It was a little funny."

She shook her head. "No. It wasn't."

He leaned in and kissed her. "Are you sure?"

"Kiss me again while I think about it." He kissed her again. "You're right. It was hilarious."

"Thank you." He patted her on the bottom and sat at the table. "It'd be a lot easier to pop corn on the stove. Or better yet, the microwave."

"But not nearly as fun. You'll eat some, right?" Without waiting for him to answer, she left the kitchen and returned a few minutes later with the cast iron corn popper. It had been hanging on the fireplace for as long as Tanner had lived there. Something left over from Winston.

It had a long handle and a lid hinged in the middle. The sides were designed to lift up as the pot filled with popcorn. She set it on the counter. "So, oil and kernels, right?"

He shrugged. "Sounds right. You might want to wash it first, though."

She gave it a quick wash and dry, then went to the pantry and returned with a jar of kernels. She got some cooking oil from the cupboard above the stove, then she poured some in the pot. She studied the jar of kernels for a moment before adding some to the pot?

"How much do you think?"

"Quarter cup. Something like that. Not too much."

She poured some more in. "That should be good."

Tanner stood. "So, now I have to go start a fire?"

"Oh, yeah. That's probably a good idea."

He went to the living room and set up the kindling with some wadded newspaper, then put two smaller pieces of firewood on top of it. He struck a match and set the paper on fire.

Harper came up behind him with the popper and he glanced at her. "It'll take a few minutes to get going." He stood. "I'm going to go take a quick shower. Don't start without me."

"Yes, sir." She watched him head for the stairs. "Do you need me to scrub your back?"

"If you did that, we'd never get the popcorn popped. I'll be down in fifteen."

When Tanner came back downstairs, the fire was going nicely. He was wearing pajama pants and a t-shirt.

Harper smiled. "Look at you, all ready for bed." She got up from the chair. "Now I need to go get on my pajamas."

"Harper."

"I'll be right back."

Tanner went to the kitchen and got a beer from the refrigerator, then returned to the living room and set two big cushions on the floor in front of it. Harper came out looking cute in plaid pajama pants and a tank top.

They sat on the cushions, and Tanner picked up the popper. "Okay, here goes."

After a few minutes, the oil started spattering inside the pot. A couple of minutes later, they heard the first pop. The popping increased, and then became non-stop. When the sides of the lid started lifting, Harper squealed.

"It's going to overflow."

"Shit." Tanner pulled the pot off the flames and set it on the hearth. The popping continued, and the popcorn overflowed onto the hearth, with an occasional piece flying through the air. Harper ducked behind Tanner.

He turned his back to the weaponized popper and put his arms around Harper, then pushed her to the floor. Harper was giggling as Tanner leaned over her.

He grinned at her. "I'd say the damn thing works."

"I think I put too many kernels in it."

"Really? You think so?" The popping slowed down, and Tanner glanced over his shoulder. When it stopped, he started to get up, but Harper grabbed the front of his t-shirt and stopped him.

"Where do you think you're going?"

He picked up a stray piece of popcorn lying on the rug next to her and put it in his mouth. "Mmm. Pretty good."

Harper put her arms around his neck and pulled him down for a kiss. "The popcorn will keep."

———— ❧ ————

Tanner and Harper were lying on the couch, sharing a blanket and a bowl of popcorn. He sighed. "I'm pretty sure this is the best popcorn I've ever tasted."

She fed him a piece, then kissed him. "I think you're right."

"Too bad my beer is all the way over there."

Harper glanced at Tanner's beer sitting on the floor near the fireplace. "I'll get it for you." She stood, taking the blanket with her.

"Hey." He grabbed a throw pillow and put it in front of him.

She picked up the beer and shook her head. "You're shy? Really?"

"Just bring me the beer."

She handed him the beer, then removed his pillow and tossed it before sitting next to him and giving him part of the blanket. She laid her head on his shoulder.

"I'm rather enjoying our secret relationship."

"It's going to get out."

"Not if we're careful."

"How's business looking?"

"Not bad. Things are picking up. Thanks to you and your family putting out the word that I'm not a witch or an interloper."

Tanner brushed some hair back from her face. "I'm not so sure about the witch part. You've got me mesmerized."

"Do you think I put a spell on you?"

"I wouldn't be surprised. One day we're frenemies and the next thing I know, we're having sex on the living room floor."

"And in my room. And in your room. And..." She smiled. "The shower."

"Like I said. Mesmerized."

"And oh, the kitchen. Well, almost the kitchen."

"I get it."

It'd been a crazy week, and Tanner had enjoyed every minute of it. Harper was enthusiastic and playful. He'd never been with anyone like her. They'd almost gotten caught kissing a few times in the barn. And Abby came into the kitchen one morning when Tanner was still in Harper's room. The secrecy added to the excitement, and the sex was amazing. He could go on like this forever. But he knew, sooner or later, they'd get caught in a compromising position. It wouldn't change much. He'd still find her just as irresistible and seemingly insatiable. Yeah. He was having a great time with Harper.

When the popcorn and his beer were gone, Tanner sighed. "I need to go check on Mister Ed."

Harper giggled. "That's his name?"

"Yes."

"Maybe you'll finally get one to talk back to you."

He kissed her shoulder. "They all talk to me. Your magic just doesn't include animal communication."

"Maybe you could teach me."

"Nah. You have to be born with it."

"You know that for a fact?"

"Yeah."

"You're full of it, my dear."

"Hey, it's the only thing I have. I'm not going to share my one thing."

"Talking to animals is only one of your many talents."

He grinned at her. "Give me a couple of others."

She thought for a moment. "You make really good popcorn."

"Yeah."

"And you're...really, really cute."

"That's not a talent."

She thought some more. "Hmm."

He pushed her onto the couch and laid on top of her. "How about I know just where to touch you to make you..." She kissed him.

"That is certainly a talent."

"I'd show you how good I am at it, but I need to go check on Mr. Ed."

She sighed and held onto him when he tried to get up. "Don't go."

"I'll be right back."

"Can we discuss some more of your talents when you come back?"

"Yes. We can. And we'll talk about a few of yours, too."

She let go of him and he sat up. "Hurry back."

"I'll meet you in your bedroom."

"Are you going to get dressed first before you go to the barn?"

"I thought I might."

"Good." She sat up. "Carry on."

He stood and put on his pajama pants, then slipped on his t-shirt. "Can I go now?"

"Yes. We'll reverse the process when you get back."

He pointed at her. "You stay just the way you are. It'll save some time."

Chapter Twenty-Three

"Quit being so impossible."

When Abby came into the kitchen at nine a.m., she was surprised to find neither Tanner nor Harper in it. But even stranger was the fact there wasn't any coffee made. She went into the living room and noticed Harper's bedroom door was opened. They might have gone into town for breakfast, but Tanner still would've made coffee. He didn't do anything before his first cup of coffee.

As she turned to go back to the kitchen, she heard Harper talking upstairs. She watched as Harper headed down the stairs in a lacy, black camisole and matching underwear. Halfway down, Harper spotted Abby.

Abby smiled. "I thought maybe you guys had gotten kidnapped."

Harper continued down the stairs. "Um...no."

"So..." Abby's smiled turned into a grin. "How long has this been going on? I knew it was. I just didn't have any proof. Until now."

Harper pointed at her room. "Let me go get some pants on."

"Good idea."

Tanner appeared at the top of the stairs in his boxers. He froze when he saw Abby. "Shit."

Abby laughed. "You need to go put pants on, too. Then come down here and we'll chat."

Tanner looked down at his boxers before turning and going back into the room. As he did, Harper came out of hers.

She smiled at Abby. "I guess the cat's out of the bag."

Abby headed for the kitchen. "Let's make some coffee. I have a feeling my little brother is going to need some."

When Tanner came into the kitchen, Harper and Abby were sitting at the table. He poured himself a cup of coffee and sat down with them and took a sip.

"Remember about seven years ago when I caught you getting Skyler a snack in the middle of the night and you asked me not to say anything?"

"I do. And you didn't. It didn't get out until the next morning when Deacon caught Skyler coming down the ladder."

Harper laughed. "Oh my. That must've been interesting."

"Fortunately, Deacon is cooler than he'd like the world to believe he is."

"So, he didn't pull the big brother card and send Skyler packing?"

"No. He invited Skyler to breakfast." She smiled at Tanner. "I don't know why you're keeping this to yourselves, but I won't tell anyone if you don't want me to."

Tanner raised an eyebrow. "Even Skyler?"

"Well, he already knew. We both did."

Tanner sighed. "We're just..."

"Keeping it to yourselves, that's fine. So, when did it start? I need all the details."

Tanner leaned back. "You're not getting details." He stood and saw Harper and Abby exchange a look. "I saw that." He looked at Harper. "It was your idea to keep a low profile."

"But she knows. Don't worry, I won't tell her anything you wouldn't want her to hear."

Tanner filled his cup again and put his hat on. "I'll be out in the barn."

"You haven't eaten."

"I'll eat later, after you two have your little hen party."

Tanner left the kitchen to the sound of the two women laughing. He crossed the yard and went into the barn. Skyler was there saddling one of the horses they were training to jump. He nodded at Tanner.

"Morning."

"Morning."

Skyler looked at him. "What's up?"

"Nothing."

"Did my wife say something she shouldn't have?"

"No. She and Harper are in the kitchen gossiping."

"Sounds about right. They've become pretty good friends."

"Yeah."

"Do you have a problem with that?"

Tanner tried to check his attitude. "No. Sorry. I love my sister."

Skyler laughed. "And she loves you."

Tanner leaned against the stall. "I might as well come clean with you, because Abby's just going to come blabbing to you, anyway."

Skyler turned to him. "Okay. What's up?"

"Harper and I are..."

"Together? Yeah. I know."

"Dammit. How?"

"We spend every day with you, man. We know you."

"So, what do you think about it?"

Skyler smiled. "It's great. What do you think about it?"

"I think it's great, too." He took a sip of coffee. "Really, really great."

"Fireworks great?"

"Oh yeah."

Skyler nodded. "Okay. Let's get this horse over to the arena."

Harper gave Abby just enough details to satisfy her. She didn't really want too many, considering they were talking about her little brother.

Abby got up and refilled her cup. "I'm really happy for you guys. Tanner has been lone- wolfing it for a while now."

"I think he was a little afraid he might catch the Carmichael trend of meet them, marry them, and start having babies."

"I'm sure he was." She sipped her coffee. "Has he told you about the gala, yet?"

"He said it's the one time of year the Carmichaels act like the royalty they are."

"That sums it up pretty well. I used to hate it. But I've gone every year since I was eighteen."

"Why do you ask?"

"I thought you might like to attend. You could get to know some of the people with money around here."

Harper nodded. "Might be good for business."

"Yeah. And you and Tanner might have fun."

"I believe we would. I'll tell him you told me about it. That should make him feel guilty."

"I told him a couple of weeks ago he should ask you."

"Well, this is Tanner we're talking about."

"Yay. I can't wait. He's never brought anyone to the gala. So, you'd be the first. And it's formal. So if you need help finding a dress, I'm your gal."

"I'll definitely need your help. I've actually never been to a formal affair."

Abby cocked her head. "Really? No high school prom?"

"I graduated before I got to it."

"Right. The smart girl. They should've let you go, anyway."

"I really wasn't interested."

"Well, that will make it even more exciting for you. The guys all dress up too. I have to admit, the Carmichael men are quite a sight on gala night. Not to mention my Fremont man, of course."

"I'm sure they will be gloriously handsome. I bet the local women were kind of upset when your brothers married women from out of town."

"They'd all given up on Deacon, because he'd sworn off women. But Tobias left a few broken hearts behind."

"And how about you?"

"I didn't date much. Kind of hard with three brothers. Not many guys found me interesting enough to go up against the Carmichael brothers. But that was fine, because no one interested me until I ran into Skyler again at the gala nine years ago. He'd just come back from Harvard."

"Impressive."

She sighed. "Yeah. He is." She smiled at Harper. "Tanner only dated one girl in high school."

"The twin?"

"Yes. Hallie. And since then, he's kind of thrown himself into the business here." She shrugged. "I'm sure he's dated. But he's pretty secretive about it."

"He is pretty dedicated to the horses. As are you."

"I kind of slid a little since I've had the girls. Skyler and Tanner carry the load these days."

"Well, having two little ones is a job in itself."

"Fortunately, I have a husband who is a very hands on dad."

"That's nice. You're lucky to have him. And so are they."

Abby stood. "Speaking of horses. I should get to work."

"Thanks, Abby."

"For what?"

"For being a good friend. I haven't really had many friends in my life. People tend to find my a bit...annoying."

Abby smiled. "That's why we get along. We're kindred souls." She headed for the door. "If you want any juicy information on my brother. I've got the scoop."

"We'll talk soon."

Tanner and Skyler worked with the horse for a couple of hours until Tanner left to get something to eat. He made himself some scrambled eggs with a few added ingredients, and when he'd finished eating, he went to the clinic. Harper was trying to stitch up a wound on a scraggly dog, who wasn't cooperating.

She looked at Tanner when he came through the door. "Come help me, please. This guy has a case of the wiggles."

Tanner moved to the examination table and held the dog still while she sutured his leg. "What happened?"

"He got hit by a car."

"Dammit."

"Yeah. Someone found him on the side of the road and brought him in. Whoever hit him didn't stop."

"Bastards."

"Do you recognize him? I don't know who he belongs to."

"If no one comes in to claim him, you can put up a flyer at the post office. Everyone has to go check their mail."

"Good idea." She glanced at him. "Don't worry, I didn't give Abby any salacious details."

"I know."

"She's really happy for us."

"Are you happy for us?"

She took her final stitch, then looked at him. "What do you mean?"

"I don't want to sneak around anymore."

She wrapped the dog's leg. "You can let go now." He backed away, and she lifted the dog and put him in a crate before returning to Tanner and hugging him.

"What's this about?"

"I'm sorry. I just want to be able to hold your hand when we walk down the street. Or kiss you on the corner if I want to."

She smiled and put her arms around his neck. "I want that too."

"You do?"

"Yes. So how about we make our official debut at your snobby, elitist Starlight Gala?"

He grinned. "Really? You want to go to the gala?"

"Yes. Abby said she'd help me find a dress. I've never done a formal dance thing before and I can't wait to see you all formaled up."

He grinned. "I do look pretty damn good in a suit."

She kissed him. "So are we good?"

"Yes. We'll make our introduction to society at the Starlight Gala."

"Sounds *so* fancy."

"Do you know how to dance?"

"Of course I know how to dance." When he raised an eyebrow, she added, "I may not technically know how to dance."

He pulled her into a dance position. "I'll give you a lesson."

"There's no music."

"We don't need music. Just do what I do in reverse."

"Huh?"

He laughed. "Okay, more simple. Sway to the music."

She looked at him. "There's no music."

"Harper. Quit being so impossible."

She grinned. "But you like it when I'm impossible."

He sighed, then pulled her in for a kiss. "Tonight, we'll practice with music."

"Thank you." She glanced at the dog. "If no one claims him, can we keep him?"

"Harper, if you keep every damn stray you come across, we'll end up with a houseful of dogs and cats."

"And?"

Tanner turned to look at the dog. "He is kind of cute."

"I'm going to call him Sebastian."

"Why?"

"I don't know. He just looks like a Sebastian to me."

"Sebastian it is."

Chapter Twenty-Four

"So, do we address you as Dr. Dolittle or Noah?"

T anner didn't often go out of town, but Skyler really wanted him to come to a horse auction in Amarillo, so they went together and spent the weekend. No one had claimed Sebastian despite Harper's efforts to find his owners, so Tanner knew when he went home he'd find three dogs in his kitchen. What he didn't expect was to find a fourth animal there.

He came through the kitchen door and dropped his leather tote on the table as the three dogs came to greet him. It took him a moment to notice another critter lying in the corner which now belonged to the dogs. He cocked his head and studied the animal.

Harper came into the kitchen and hugged him. "I missed you."

Tanner gave her a distracted kiss. "Why is there a fawn in our kitchen?"

Harper smiled at the fawn who could only be a few days old. "That's Fiona."

Tanner took a moment to consider the name. "Fiona the fawn. Cute. But that doesn't answer my question."

Harper took his arm and led him to the table, then gently pushed him into a chair before going to the refrigerator and getting him a beer. He opened it, took a sip, then looked at her.

She sat down. "Randy found her in the brush near the hay shed. Her mother was dead, and Fiona was barely alive. He brought her to me, because he couldn't just leave her to die."

"So, you saved her."

"Yes."

"And now she's in the kitchen."

"I couldn't leave her in the clinic by herself. It's cold, and she'd be all alone." The dogs returned to their corner and laid by the fawn. "See, the boys love her."

Tanner started laughing. "You can't keep her. She's a wild animal."

Harper got up and went to the fawn, then sat next to her. The fawn laid her head on Harper's lap. "She thinks I'm her mother."

"Shit, Harper. You're going to have to feed her every couple of hours."

"I slept in here with her last night. She sleeps about four hours at a time."

He got up and sat next to Harper and the fawn. He gave it a pet, then smiled at Harper. "Good thing we have a big damn house."

"So, I can keep her?"

"Like you'd listen to me if I said you couldn't."

She hugged him. "Isn't she adorable?"

"Yes. She's adorable."

Even though he'd only been gone two days, Tanner had missed Harper and by the time they ate dinner and did the dishes, he was impatiently waiting for her to feed Fiona so they could go upstairs to bed.

Harper glanced at him while she fed Fiona a bottle. "She's almost done."

Tanner scowled. "I spent the whole ride home thinking about what I wanted to do to you when I got home. This wasn't it."

Fiona finished the bottle and Harper got to her feet. "We just need to take everyone outside to go potty, then you can have your way with me."

He put his arms around her and pulled her in close, then nibbled on her ear. She giggled, and wiggled out of his grasp. "The sooner we get them walked, the sooner we can get to it."

Tanner went to the door and opened it. "Come on, you mangy bunch of animals."

The dogs all ran outside as Harper picked up Fiona and took her outside. She set her down, and they gave it ten minutes before they rounded the dogs up and went back inside. Harper put the fawn on the dog bed next to Joey.

"Okay, you guys. Get some sleep. Fiona will be up in a few hours."

Tanner took her hand. "Then let's go."

They jogged up the stairs, and Tanner stopped at the door and took Harper in his arms. "I missed you."

"Hmm. I missed you too, cowboy."

He led her into the room as he took off his t-shirt and unbuckled his belt. He sat on the bed and Harper pulled off his boots, then straddled his lap and put her arms around his neck. "Do you think we'll ever get to a point where the fireworks stop?"

He shook his head and kissed her. "Never."

"Good. I'm rather enjoying the fireworks."

He laid back, bringing her with him. "Let's go for the grand finale again."

"Mmm. My favorite."

———————— ❈ ————————

When the bed moved, Tanner opened his eyes and reached for Harper's hand. "Where are you going?"

"I have to feed Fiona."

He sighed. "Hurry back."

When she didn't return in a reasonable amount of time, Tanner went down to the kitchen to see what was keeping her. He found Harper curled up on the floor next to the fawn, sound asleep. He went to her room and grabbed two pillows and some blankets, and brought them to the kitchen.

He shook her gently. "Hey."

She looked up at him. "I fell asleep."

He handed her a pillow and a blanket, then laid down next to her. "We'll stay here with Fiona for a while."

She smiled as she snuggled into the pillow. "You're the best."

He put his arm over her. "I know."

———————— ❈ ————————

Abby and Skyler came into the kitchen and stopped when they saw Harper and Tanner asleep on the floor. Tanner heard them and rolled over to look at them.

"Shit. It's morning?"

Abby smiled. "Yeah it is. Is this some sort of weird animal thing you got going on here? Because we can leave you to it."

He sat with a grunt, which woke up Harper. She smiled. "Hey guys."

Abby spotted Fiona. "Is that a fawn?"

Tanner looked at Fiona. "Yep." He got slowly to his feet and stretched out his back, then got out of the way as Abby moved in to see the baby up close.

"Oh my gosh, she's adorable."

Tanner sighed and looked at Skyler, who smiled. "Welcome to fatherhood."

Tanner flipped him off and started the coffee maker, then leaned on the counter and yawned. Skyler sat at the table and Abby glanced at him. "Don't you want to come pet this beautiful thing?"

He held up his hand. "No, I'm good."

When the coffee was finished, Tanner filled three cups and handed one to Skyler, then set one on the table for Abby. He resumed leaning on the counter while he drank from the third cup.

Skyler took a sip of his coffee. "So, do we address you as Dr. Dolittle or Noah?"

"I'm not sure yet. Give it a little more time. So far they've only come to us one at a time."

Harper got to her feet. "Time for this baby to eat. Do you want to feed her, Abby?"

"Yes, please."

Tanner smiled at Harper. "Time for this baby to eat, too."

She cocked her head. "You know I'm not going to cook you bacon and eggs."

He nodded. "I can always hope."

He let her prepared the bottle for Fiona, then took a carton of eggs and a package of bacon from the refrigerator. "Did you guys eat?"

Skyler grinned. "I can always eat bacon and eggs."

Abby took the bottle from Harper. "I'll take some bacon."

Harper kissed Tanner on the cheek. "While you all eat your animal products, I'm going to go take a shower."

"Don't use all the hot water."

"I'll try not to."

He pointed at her. "I'm serious. I spent the night on the kitchen floor with you, three dogs, and a fawn. I need a shower before I go to work."

She smiled and blew him a kiss. "I'll be very conservative."

Harper had a fairly full morning, with three office visits and two house calls. She and Abby were driving to Amarillo right after lunch to find dresses for the gala. They'd be home late, so Tanner would be left in charge of feeding Fiona.

He went to see her in the clinic before she left. "I don't remember volunteering to babysit a fawn while you're gone."

She gave him a hug. "But you'll do it, because you love animals as much as I do."

"How much do I give her, and how often?"

"I just fed her, so again around four and eight. Fill the bottle with formula to the line in the middle. It's premixed in the refrigerator. Warm it up, but not too hot. I should be home for the midnight feeding."

"I should hope so. I don't want you driving home that late."

She smiled at him. "Are you going to worry about me?"

"Yes."

She hugged him again. "That's sweet. I never had anyone worry about me before."

"I'm sure your parents worried about you."

"Well, sure. And my brother. But not someone like..."

"A boyfriend?"

"Yeah."

He kissed her. "Go already, so you can get back."

"I promise you, the dress will be worth the worry."

"It better be."

He watched her go, then went to the stall to see Fiona. She was asleep, but he was afraid she'd wake up and get scared when she found herself alone. He went to the barn door and whistled for Rider. The dog came bounding up with Sebastian lagging a bit behind on his injured leg. Little Joey brought up the rear.

"Come on, you guys. You're on babysitting duty with me. I've got a horse to train."

The dogs all went into the stall with Fiona and laid down next to her. Tanner watched them for a moment, then left to go get some work done.

When Harper came into the kitchen a few minutes past eight, Tanner was sitting at the table with Fiona in his lap. He was feeding her while eating a bowl of stew. Harper hugged him from behind and kissed his cheek.

"You are the most adorable man ever."

She picked up Fiona and took over the feeding. "Has she been a good girl?"

"Yes. I only had to put her in timeout once."

She kissed Fiona's nose. "Good girl."

"How'd the dress shopping go?"

She set Fiona down and put the bottle in the sink. "You are going to be very impressed."

"Oh yeah?"

"Yeah. And Abby told me you have a gray suit. So, it'd be really cool if you wore it."

"I was planning on it."

"Good." She left the kitchen and came back with a shopping bag. "Because I got you a tie."

"You got me a tie?"

"Yes. A tie that will compliment my dress."

She pulled it out of the bag and showed it to him.

He took it from her. It was light gray with thin purple stripes. "You got me a purple tie."

"It's not purple. It's gray with a tiny bit of purple."

He smiled. "I love it. Thank you."

"So, you'll wear it?"

"Of course."

He looked at Fiona. "The question is, what's Fiona going to wear?"

Chapter Twenty-Five

"It's been a wonderful nine years."

T anner was coming down the stairs when Harper came out of her room. He stopped halfway down when he saw her.

"Wow."

"Wow, yourself."

She continued down to the bottom of the stairs, then crossed the room to her. She ran a hand over his lapels.

"This is very nice." She straightened his tie. "The tie is great."

"Don't get used to it. I only wear a suit once a year to the gala. Unless someone gets married. But seeing as all my siblings have tied the knot, I'm good."

"Well, you wear it well."

"You don't look half bad yourself."

"Abby helped."

"Your dress matches your hair." She patted her hair.

He leaned back and looked at her. "And where are those adorable glasses of yours?"

"It thought I'd look more..."

"Go get them."

"Really?"

"Yes. I love your glasses."

She sighed. "Oh good. Because I can't see a thing." She ran back to her room and came back out with her glasses on. She stopped a few feet in front of Tanner. "Even more impressive now that I can actually see you."

He took her arm. "Come on, you weirdo."

"Weirdo?"

"Yes. My weirdo. We're going to be late."

She resisted when he tried to lead her to the door. "Am I going to make a fool of myself?"

"Of course not. Why would you think that?"

"I'm just so out of my element."

"Harper. You're going to a party attended by people who spend every other day of the year in jeans and cowboy boots." He ran a hand down his suit jacket. "This is just a costume."

"Okay. You're right." They headed for the door. "Maybe you could wear it for Halloween."

"I'm not wearing a suit for Halloween."

"I could wear my dress and we could go as the king and queen of the gala."

Tanner opened the door for her. "There is no king and queen."

"What about Deacon?"

"He's not a king. He's a tyrant."

When they got to the truck, she looked at it. "Did you wash the truck?"

"Of course. I can't take my queen to the gala in a dirty truck." He opened the door for her and helped her in, then went around and got in behind the wheel. "My mother always insisted on using the Escalade and a driver, so the Carmichael family arrive at the same time."

"That's kind of cute. I guess."

"Once everyone started getting married and living in different houses, it was a little inconvenient."

"Do you miss living at home with everybody?"

He thought about the question. "No. I did at first. But I like having my privacy. Of course, I don't know if I can call it privacy when Abby and Skyler come and go as they please."

"They've been more respectful of that since they found out we were...together."

"You cleaned that up nicely."

"Well, tonight I'm a lady." She took his hand. "Do you think Fiona will be okay?"

"Riley will take good care of her. He has a timer set to get up and feed her."

"But she's alone in the barn."

"She's not alone. She has ten horses to keep her company. Plus I took Rider over with Fiona. She'll be fine. You can't begrudge Ruthie not wanting a fawn in her kitchen."

Harper smiled. "I guess not."

"I'm sure Thea will help him, too. All the kids were very excited to meet her."

So, they're having a giant sleepover at the main house?"

"Yes. The nanny and Ruthie have it all under control."

"Okay."

"Can we go now?"

"Yes. We can go. I'm just a little nervous."

He kissed the side of her head. "You'll be fine."

———————— ❧ ————————

Over the years, Deacon had become more relaxed during the Starlight Gala, but he still fell into obsessive Mr. Carmichael once in a while. He was on the verge of berating a young man over a tray full of dirty cups sitting on a hundred-and-fifty-year-old side table when Cassidy came up and took his arm.

"Mr. Carmichael." She smiled at the man dressed in a uniform. "Thank you, David." He nodded and picked up the tray before dashing off with it.

Deacon smiled at her. "Hello, schoolteacher."

She put her arm through his. "I thought we were past Deacon Carmichael the—"

"Asshole?"

She laughed. "I was going to say dictator. But yes."

"I think I prefer asshole."

She looked around the room. "Everyone is happy. No one is complaining about trays of cups being left lying around. It's all good."

"Hmm." He kissed her forehead. "Thanks to you. You have become the perfect host. Rivaling my mother, even."

"That's quite a compliment. Now, come dance with me."

"Yes, ma'am." They moved to the dance floor and Deacon took Cassidy in his arms. "The first time I danced with you, I was so confused."

"How so?"

"You instantly made me feel things I didn't want to feel. And there was the whole, Tobias being in love with you thing. And you had mentioned a boyfriend when I met you at Tanner's school. So, a lot of things to be confused about."

"Well, I'm glad you worked through all that."

"It has been a wonderful nine years."

"It went so fast."

"Having kids will do that."

Cassidy laid her head on his shoulder. "You know that thing we've been wondering about for the last six weeks?"

"You mean the..."

"Yes. I believe it's time to take the test."

He pulled back and looked at her. "Baby number five?"

She laughed. "We really need to stop at some point, you know."

"Maybe. But five is an uneven number. So we have to have at least one more after this one."

She smiled at him. "You tell everyone I'm the one who loves kids. But you and I both know it's you who's behind this growing family of ours."

Deacon shrugged. "What can I say? We're so good at it."

Tobias approached them and grinned. "I need my wingman. Time to improve the punch."

Deacon kissed Cassidy, then stepped away from her. "Go make your welcome speech. We need a distraction."

"Like everyone here doesn't know Tobias spikes the punch every year."

"Just humor me. Let us go on pretending they have no idea how it happened."

She nodded, then headed for the four-piece orchestra who was supplying the music.

Deacon watched her say something to the musicians, then he put a hand on Tobias' shoulder. "Okay, let's do this."

As the music stopped and Cassidy began to welcome everyone, they headed for the table with a huge crystal punch bowl and matching cups set out in neat rows beside it. The young woman behind the table got instantly nervous when she spotted the two impressive Carmichael men headed for her.

She gave Deacon a nervous smile. "Mr. Carmichael."

Tobias leaned in toward Deacon's ear. "Is she talking to you or me?"

Deacon nudged him, then nodded toward the tray of used glasses. "Do you think my guests want to see a tray full of dirty cups?"

"No sir." She picked up the tray and headed for the kitchen.

Tobias pulled a fifth of rum from his jacket pocket and Deacon patted his shoulder. "Carry on. I know nothing."

Tobias watched him leave, then emptied the bottle into the punch. He stirred it with the ladle, then poured himself a cup. As he took a sip, Gemma came up to him.

"Am I too late to get myself some punch?"

He took her arm and gasped as he swallowed some punch. "Definitely too late. Let's get out of here."

She looked at him. "You are aware everyone around here knows you spike the punch, right?"

"Yeah, yeah. I know." He grinned. "But nobody lets on they know. It's tradition, and it's worked that way since I was sixteen."

"That's when you started? How did you get the alcohol?"

"Deacon. It was the first gala after my dad died. He was still cool back then."

"Deacon is cool now, too. And I know you realize that."

He kissed her and patted her stomach. "Don't ruin my thing."

"Fine. Will you dance with your pregnant wife?"

They went to the dance floor and started dancing. "That gala nine years ago, when I was chasing after Cassidy and Deacon was pretending he didn't care, I had a second bottle of rum with me. I spent a fair amount of time drinking it in one of the private rooms."

"Those days are behind you now."

"Thanks to you." He kissed her. "My own private physical therapist."

"Once you started listening to me."

"After this dance, I have something to show you."

"What?"

"It's a surprise. A Happy Eighth Gala gift of sorts."

"Well, I can't wait through this dance to find out." She stepped away from him and led him off the dance floor and out into the garden.

She stopped walking, but he took her hand and continued on. "Let's go to the secret garden." They went to the garden in the middle of a circle of Italian Cypress trees. There was no one there and Tobias took Gemma to the table in the middle of the space and sat her down.

He stayed on his feet and took a few steps back from her. "So, do you remember the Malady Springs motel?" She cocked her head, and he grinned. "Just kidding. I heard a few months back they were selling the place."

"Oh no."

He smiled and pulled a piece of paper out of his pocket. "Yeah. I was afraid no one would want it and the place would shut down." He handed the paper to her. "So, I bought it. We bought it. We own the Malady Springs Motel."

Gemma looked at the paper, then stood and hugged him. "I can't believe you did this."

"I couldn't have our favorite yearly honeymoon spot close down. Where would we go? Hawaii? The Bahamas?"

"You're crazy, Tobias Carmichael. But I love you. This is the best present ever."

"I was going to give it to you for Christmas, but I couldn't wait."

"We're going to leave it just the way it is, right?"

"Yes. And the Franklin's are staying on to run the place."

"What about the bar? I thought both places were owned by the same person."

"They are. They're both owned by us now. I made our favorite bartender the bar manager."

Abby and Skyler were sitting at a table in the garden. Abby reached for his hand. "This is where we were sitting when your mother dragged you away so she could show you off to her friends."

"She wanted to find me a suitable wife. That Carmichael girl monopolizing all of my time wasn't quite what she had in mind."

"Well, we showed her, didn't we?" He gave her a smile, then lost it when he spotted something behind her. "What?" She turned to see Leo and Helen headed their way. "Whoa. Talk about weird déjà vu."

Skyler got to his feet as Abby stood next to him and took his arm possessively. "Mom." Helen hesitated before giving him a stiff, awkward hug. He looked at his father. "Dad."

Leo nodded.

"What are you doing here?"

"I believe we're on the guest list."

"Of course. But you've been on it for the last seven years and you haven't attended."

Leo cleared his throat. "We wanted to talk to you. And we figured here, you'd have to stay and listen or risk embarrassing both families."

"You figured wrong, Dad. This isn't the place to mend our broken fences. And honestly, I think they're beyond mending."

Leo glanced around at the other guests, who were watching without looking like they were watching. "Can we sit for a moment? At least give the appearance of civility?"

Skyler sighed, then motioned toward the table. The four of them sat and Abby put a hand on Skyler's thigh under the table and patted it.

He glanced at her, then looked at his father. "A first step would be you acknowledging the fact Abby is my wife and the mother of my children. Your grandchildren who you've yet to meet."

Helen reached for his hand, but stopped herself and put her hands in her lap. "Every day that goes by breaks my heart a little more." She looked at Abby. "Of course we know you're Skyler's wife and the two of you have united the Carmichael and Fremont families."

Abby could tell Skyler was trying to stay strong. It'd been seven years since his father disowned him. "You haven't talked to me in seven years."

Leo cleared his throat again. "We'd like to change that. I won't ask you to forgive me. But I was hoping we could make some progress toward working through this. I realize it'll take time. I'm not asking for a miracle here. But someday, we'd like to be part of our grandchildren's lives."

Skyler sighed, then nodded. "Okay. You've said your peace." He stood. "Abby and I will consider what you've said."

Leo stood too and offered his hand. "That's all I can ask." Skyler shook with him, then Leo took Helen's arm and they left the table. Helen looked over her shoulder at them, then went off with her husband.

Abby looked at Skyler. "Are you okay?"

He smiled. "Yeah. I'm great." He took a breath. "I'm just going to let the old man stew for a while."

"And then?"

"And then the girls may finally meet their grandparents."

Chapter Twenty-Six

"So, how long has this been going on?"

T anner and Harper arrived at the gala, and when they came through the doors to the main hall, Harper stopped to take it all in. "Wow. You were right. This is pretentiousness in overdrive. Look at all these beautiful people."

Tanner looked around. "It is an impressive sight." He saw Cassidy headed his way, and he gave her a smile.

"Hey, guys. Wow, you look beautiful, Harper." Tanner cocked his head, and she added. "As do you, Tanner."

He kissed her cheek. "And you are lovely as always. Where's your husband?"

"Oh, he's around here somewhere. Harassing a waiter, or telling the musicians how to play." She shrugged. "He just can't help himself."

"And ah...has Tobias fulfilled his gala duty?"

"Yes. The punch has been made better."

Tanner laughed. "We'll have to give it a try." He looked around the room. "You've outdone yourself this year."

"It's really a joint effort between Gemma and I. I never felt right taking on the roll as Supreme Hostess of the Starlight Gala."

"So, you're Supreme Co-hostess now?"

"Yes. And I feel much better about it." She gave him a hug. "Now I need to go track down the Supreme Host."

She wandered off, and Harper took Tanner's arm. "So are we going to make an announcement or is me being on your arm enough to let everyone know we're an item?"

"That and all the dancing I'm planning on doing with you."

"Are you sure we practiced enough?"

"You'll be fine."

"First, maybe we should check out the famous spiked punch I've heard so much about."

"Trust me. It won't help your dancing. But it might make you care less about what people think."

"Well, it's tradition, right? Part of the experience?"

"I suppose."

"Then let's go get some."

"Okay. Don't say I didn't warn you."

They crossed the room as they headed to the big table with the crystal punch bowl. They were stopped by several people, and Tanner introduced Harper to the ones she didn't know. He didn't specifically introduce her as his girlfriend, but he kept hold of her hand the whole time.

When they arrived at the punch bowl, the girl behind the table nodded and gave them a smile.

"Hi Tanner."

"Becky. How's it going?"

"Your brother has only reprimanded me once, so not too bad."

"Don't let him get to you. He's all bark."

"I know. Plus, the money we get paid is totally worth it."

Tanner nodded, and Harper whispered into his ear. "Another girl-friend?"

He shook his head and picked up two cups, then handed one to Harper. "Thanks, Becky." He looked at Harper. "Take it slow."

She sipped some punch. "Whoa!"

"I told you."

"No. It's good." She took another sip. "What's in it?"

"Rum."

"Interesting. I've never had rum."

He took a step back from her. "How is that possible?"

"I told you. Margaritas." She finished her punch and held it out to be refilled.

Tanner waited for Becky to refill the cup. Then he took Harper's arm and pulled her away from the table. "You need to pace yourself with the punch. It'll sneak up on you."

She sipped from her refilled cup and he frowned. "How can you like rum and not beer?"

"This has fruity stuff in it." She looked around the room at the closed doors along the edges of the grand hall. "What's behind the doors?"

"Off limits."

"Even for a Carmichael?"

"We host the gala. But we don't own the Connelly House."

"Still, as host..."

"No. Off limits."

"We can't even take a peek?"

He laughed. "You're like a kid. Someone tells you no, and you want it even more."

"Just one peek through one door."

Tanner looked at the doors. "Okay. The one behind the punch bowl seems the least conspicuous. And Becky will cover for us."

"So she is an old girlfriend."

He took her arm, and they returned to the punch bowl table. They set their empty glasses down, then Tanner smiled at Becky. "We're going to take a look in this room. If someone comes looking for me, will you steer them somewhere else?"

"Sure."

Tanner looked around, and when no one seemed to be looking their way, he opened the door and pushed Harper through it.

The room had been an office at one point and was furnished with an antique desk, several bookshelves, and two chairs by a stone fireplace. Harper looked around. "Wow. This is amazing. Did people named Connelly actually live here?"

"Yes. They founded the town."

"Were they ranchers?"

"No. Oilman. There was a tiny town here called Hooker Basin."

"Lovely name."

"Not that kind of hooker. Hooker creek used to run through town. Named after John Hooker. The water got diverted when they built the dam and formed the lake."

"And Mr. Connelly built himself a big, beautiful house?"

"Yep. And made himself mayor."

"How soon after did the pesky Carmichaels arrive and start buying up the valley?"

"Connelly was still mayor when my great grandfather settled the first 40,000 acres."

Harper went to him and put her arms around his neck. "That's super interesting and all, but I really wanted to come in here so I could kiss you."

He pulled her in close. "Hmm. I thought we weren't hiding behind closed doors anymore."

"We're not. But I'm not going to make out with Prince Tanner on the dance floor. I'm a lady, after all."

He kissed her. "Good, because I'm ready to let everyone know how much I love you."

She leaned back. "You love me?"

"Have I not made that clear?"

She hugged him, then kissed him. "I love you too, my handsome cowboy. But I was afraid to say it. I didn't want to ruin things."

He frowned at her. "How would that ruin things?"

"Well, if you didn't feel the same way, then it'd get awkward." She smiled. "I'm really glad you love me."

Tanner pulled Harper in close and kissed her again. While the fireworks were going off around them, he heard the familiar sound of his brother clearing his throat. He stepped away from Harper and turned to see Deacon standing inside the doorway.

"Sorry to interrupt."

Tanner glanced at Harper. "Yeah. Um..."

Deacon raised an eyebrow. "How long has this been going on?"

"A couple of months."

"So, about the time Harper moved into the house?"

"Not right away, no. A couple of weeks after that."

Deacon grinned. "You realize we all know, right?"

Tanner scowled. "No way. Did Abby tell you? She swore she wouldn't."

"No. Abby didn't tell me."

"Am I that transparent?"

"You know you're not supposed to be in here. These rooms are off-limits, even to us. They're afraid we might damage something irreplaceable."

"We were just..."

"I saw what you were just." He nodded at Harper. "Welcome to the family, Harper."

Tanner took a step forward. "We're not..." He glanced at Harper. "Well..." He smiled. "Maybe we are."

She took his arm. "This was my idea. Coming into the room. I talked him into it."

"I'm pretty sure Tanner doesn't do anything he doesn't want to do." Deacon glanced toward the door. "Your friend Becky gave you up. But don't be upset with her. I gave her my best stern Deacon Carmichael look." He headed for the door. "I've got to go do what I do. You two...carry on."

Deacon left the room, and Tanner returned to Harper and pulled her in close. "You heard the man."

She looked at him. "I really like your brother."

"Yeah. He's great."

"Seriously. He's—"

"Harper. Did we come in here to make out? Or did we come in here to talk about how great my brother is?"

She smiled. "We came in here to make out. But don't touch anything. I don't want to damage anything irreplaceable."

"I'm not planning on touching anything but you."

After some serious kissing, they moved to the black velvet settee and sat down. Tanner put his arm around Harper and she laid her head on his shoulder.

"We probably shouldn't be sitting on this couch."

"It's fine. We're not going to hurt it."

"I wonder how old it is?"

Tanner sighed. "Harper."

"Sorry." She put a hand on his chest. "How many times have you been in love?"

He thought about the question. "I thought I was in love with Hallie. But now I know I wasn't. So the answer would be once, with you."

She tilted her head up and smiled at him. "Once for me, too."

"With?"

"You of course."

"Just checking. It's...kind of nice, huh?"

"Yes. It's kind of nice."

"Now I know why my brothers got weird and kind of crazy when they fell in love. It makes you want to do stupid stuff."

"Such as?"

"I don't know. Sleep on the kitchen floor with a baby fawn because the woman you love is ridiculously fond of animals."

"Hey, you talk to them. That makes us both a little ridiculous about animals."

"I guess you're right. We're a match made in heaven."

They were both quiet for a moment, then Harper put a hand on Tanner's thigh. "The day we met, you said you didn't want to get married."

"Did I?"

"Yes. You did."

"Hmm. Well, I guess I hadn't met the right woman."

She sat up and looked at him. "So, you've changed your mind?"

He took her hand and kissed her forehead. "Are you trying to get me to ask you to marry me?"

She shook her head. "No. I just want to know if you're open to the idea."

He was quiet again for a few moments, then pulled her in close. "Would a spring wedding suit you?"

She snuggled into his side. "I always wanted to get married at Christmastime."

Tanner laughed, then kissed the top of her head. "Am I ever going to have the last word in our relationship?"

"I always listen to what you have to say."

"Right. And then we do it your way."

"That's why you love me."

He pushed her down onto the couch and kissed her. "That's why I love you."

She put a hand on his chest. "Tanner. I don't want to have to pay for this couch."

He laughed. "We can afford it."

Together with their loving family, Tanner and Harper invite you to celebrate a Carmichael Christmas WeddingDecember 24th at the Starlight Ranch!

More Books By Leigh Fenty

The Deputy
The Best Woman
The Chief
The Family Man
The Visitor

About the Author

L eigh spends her days with cute, sexy guys. Unfortunately, they're on paper. But still, not a bad way to spend your day. She also writes about strong, independent women, who can hold their own against these irresistible guys. She's not a pure romance writer, because she breaks the rules a bit. But that's the fun part. Leigh's stories have adventure, family relationships, and the struggles life throws at you sometimes. But boy always meets girl. They tussle a bit while they figure out what they really want. Then find their happily ever after. Even if it's not what they thought it was going to be.

Printed in Great Britain
by Amazon

51190188R00126